# Summers After

Kara DeMaio

© 2021

ISBN: 978-1-7358455-7-9 (pbk.)

For more information, visit LifeTranscribed.com

For my cousin, Jenn —
who always believed I would finish this
and for being the true embodiment
of "never giving up."

I love you.

# 1 - Ayla

I glance down at my feet and realize my flip flops are filthy and wet. I must have walked through a puddle and not realized it, lost in a daze that seems to plague me lately. I shiver despite it being the dead of summer.

I continue on my journey, something that has become a bit of a routine for me. I glance down at my arms, covered in goosebumps that seem to appear every time I am close. It's been dark for a few hours now and the moon is high and bright in the sky above me. I reach for the gate and pull it open with a bit of a struggle, the heavy weight in my hands making them shake with effort. It closes behind me with a loud crash, echoing through the darkness. A calming peace spreads over me as I approach him and I soak it in like a drug. It's the feeling I've been chasing for the past two years — the feeling that I can never seem to hold onto anywhere else. He's had that effect on me since the moment I met him. As I walk up the last part of the hill, I close my eyes and breathe deeply, the scent of fresh dirt and just-cut grass hangs heavy in the air. A smile slowly finds its way across my face and I silently wish I could run up to him and jump in his arms. My heart aches at the thought.

When I'm close enough, I take my usual place on the ground facing him. I sit with my legs crossed in the wet grass, not caring that I'm wearing a dress. I instinctively reach out and place my hand on the dark stone in front of me, running my fingers across the smooth surface and tracing the letters of his name.

*It's hard to believe it's been almost two years since you left me.*

It feels like yesterday and a lifetime ago at the same time. So much has happened since, and I quickly push away the thought of how messed up things are now. Because that line of thought brings me to a dangerous place, where the memory of that night taunts me, threatening to replay on a torturous loop that doesn't end without the aid of something that helps me to forget.

I reach into the pockets of my dress and pull out the cans of beer I grabbed on the way here. I open both quickly, the soft pop making my mouth water. I sit one in front of the stone and then tilt mine to my mouth, allowing the now slightly warm beer to fall down my throat without tasting it. I finish more than half of it with the first few gulps. I smile and clink my can to his, a toast to him that I'm not sure he's aware of. I close my eyes and try to imagine his laugh, but I can't seem to get it right in my mind. I open my eyes again and envision him sitting across from me, laughing at me for being ridiculous, and I laugh out loud in spite of the ache in my chest.

"That's the first time I've laughed all night," I say to Tate, hoping that wherever he is he can hear me.

I proceed to tell him about the day, my latest fight with Jase this morning and the prank I played on Alex before we went out tonight.

Most people I know are out partying along the beach, drinking at a local bar or dancing in one of the clubs downtown. I attempt to do these things, too. I try to pretend that I am okay and everything is normal, but it never lasts long. Despite my best efforts to pretend that my whole world didn't change in a matter of minutes that night two years ago — to pretend my insides aren't constantly churning with loss and anger and heartache — it isn't long before all of that bubbles to the surface and I have to leave quickly before I completely lose it in front of everyone, or worse, in front of Ryan or Jase. Both of them seem to always be waiting for me to break down, dancing around me cautiously as if one wrong move may cause me to completely shatter. It drives me insane, even if they are mostly right. And so, regardless of where I am or who I am with when I do feel like I may shatter, I typically leave without so much as a word. I disappear, wishing I could actually disappear for a while, and my feet almost always bring me here even if I hadn't intended them to. I know that it drives Jase crazy that I leave him wherever we are without an explanation, because he constantly worries about me now. And while I should find that sweet, it makes me angry instead and I can't fully explain why. I also know how weird the guys think it is that I'm here, even if they won't say it out loud.

I guess the truth is that most nineteen-year-olds don't typically hang out in a cemetery at midnight, but then again, most nineteen-year-olds haven't had to watch their best friend die in their arms.

# 2 - Jase

"She's gone again," I say out loud to no one in particular.

I shake my head in Ryan's direction, but he won't meet my eyes. I swallow what's left of my drink and scan the room again. Ryan motions to the bartender for another round and when I put my hand up to stop him, he shakes his head at me. His eyes flicker with sadness and pain for only a moment before both disappear into the smile he tries to carry now. Even that seems pained though, a far stretch from the laid back, carefree grin he used to always have.

"We both know where she is — where she always ends up. Have another drink with me and then we'll head home. You know she'll be back at the house before you know it."

I know there is no point in arguing with Ryan, because for all intents and purposes, he is right. I know she is either already at the cemetery or on her way there. And yes, she almost always finds her way back to me — to all of us — eventually. She won't say it out loud, but when her eyes meet mine, I always know exactly where she's been.

I try to be understanding, but I still worry about her all of the time. Every moment she's not with me, I fear the worst. I could have lost her, too, that night two years ago, and the mere thought of that is enough to bring me to my knees. I'm not sure I'll ever know what she went through that night or all of the details of what happened before we arrived. I want to, only to help her carry some of it, but she insists on carrying it alone. She is constantly trying to prove something, although I have no idea to whom. We all lost Tate. He was like a younger brother to each of us and Ryan's actual little brother. The pain in his eyes is present every time he talks about Tate, but at least he talks about him. At least we can have conversations when he's having a tough time with it so I can try to help, even if it's only to listen.

I can't do that with Ayla. She shuts down completely, like she's flipped a switch to turn off that entire night and everything she feels about it except anger. She seems to be angry all of the time now. And that's okay. If that's what she needs to do to keep moving forward, I understand, but I also know that avoiding things usually only makes them worse. I don't want things to be any worse for her. I hate that she had to go through what she did alone. I hate that I wasn't there for her that night — that I wasn't there for both of them. I should have been. And that's my burden to carry. It's yet another regret to add to my pile.

I think about how I found her that night — wrapped around Tate so tight that you couldn't tell where she ended and he began. They were both covered in so much blood that a surge of panic locked my feet in place. I felt the world sway beneath me while something inside my chest exploded as I watched her rock him back and forth. She sounded like a wounded animal, so full of pain and so achingly sad that I knew he was gone before I moved any closer. The world stopped around us and I couldn't hear anything but her pain. I spoke to her softly at first, but I'm not sure that she heard me right away. She was lost somewhere, a distant look in her eyes that I see return often now. It looked like she was lost somewhere far away that night and it scared the hell out of me. I closed the distance between us and pulled her into my arms gently, trying to see if she was hurt. Her eyes focused once again, and she folded into me like she wanted me to hold her and never let her go. If it were up to me, I would have done just that. There are days now that I have trouble looking Ryan in the eye because of the guilt I carry for feeling relief in that moment — relief that Ayla seemed to be mostly okay once she was in my arms. But she's not really okay, even when she pretends to be.

*Who would be?*

That distant look in her eye returns often. I've become used to it now. I think she spends most of her time somewhere else. Her body is here, but her mind is lost in another place and time. She holds everything in. She's built a wall around everything that happened that night and won't let anyone inside — not even me. She used to tell me that Tate and I were the two people she was never afraid to tell anything to, but now there are days that I worry she won't ever let me in again. It's not like this all of the time. There are moments where she catches my eye, and she smiles that smile that will forever make me stop in my tracks and believe the world is right again. But I know that smile hides what she's really feeling, and I can't seem to get her to understand that it's okay to let me see what's underneath.

Don't get me wrong. We all try to pretend that everything is okay even when we all know that it's not. Some days it's easier to pretend that we can all move on and somehow be okay or that things are like they used to be. We know they never will be.

Ryan shoves a drink toward me, so I take it without argument. Ace approaches us both, asking if we know where Jesse is tonight. We shrug and shake our heads, and Ace sits down on the stool next to me, defeated.

"I give up. I can't keep track of him anymore. He stopped telling me anything."

Ace hangs his head a bit and I motion to the bartender for him. I can relate. He's going through something similar with his younger brother, Jesse, who seems lost since everything that happened to Tate. Jesse and Ayla bond now, both trying to escape things instead of dealing with them. They have their own private club that's heading down a dangerous path, but that's something else that Ayla doesn't want to hear about from me, regardless of the personal experience I have with it.

I wash away the jealous anger with another sip of whiskey as I think about the fight we had earlier today and how she went running to Jesse immediately after.

Sure, I understand wanting to escape things. I understand wanting to have a drink or two and relax with friends to unwind. I just wish she wouldn't drink as much as she does. I watched my mom do the same thing and it brings back many memories from growing up. I try not to let those memories bleed into how I respond to Ayla's drinking, but I can't keep it from seeping into the edge of every argument we have about it. She doesn't want to hear it. And now she disappears all of the time without ever saying anything to me first. It's like I'm not even here. Sometimes I think she forgets that I am. I can feel her slowly slipping away from me. Before Tate died, we never fought — ever. Things are different now. She's different now. Everything I say seems to make her angry and we're constantly frustrated with one another. She used to be the only person I could talk to about anything, and now we have trouble communicating about everything.

"Earth to Jase. Hello in there?"

I pick up my head and realize that Jessica, Ayla's friend who works for Ryan's dad, has been trying to talk to me. I hadn't noticed her walk up beside me and I hadn't heard her say anything.

*Apparently, Ayla isn't the only one lost in thought lately.*

"Sorry," I say as I smile weakly at her.

She places her hand on my arm.

"Where's A?"

A is how most people in town refer to Ayla, a loving nickname our friends had given her that spread beyond us quickly. I shrug at Jessica and shake my head slowly.

"Cemetery, I'm guessing, but she didn't mention it before she left."

*She never does.*

# 3 – Ayla

I glance over my shoulder and watch as his headstone gets smaller behind me. Every time I have to leave him, I feel like I'm leaving him behind, just like I felt the day we buried him. It strikes me that no matter how old I get, he'll always remain the same age. He's never going to celebrate another birthday. He's never going to go to college or get married or live next door to me like we planned. He's going to stay seventeen forever, rotting in a box inside the ground. A strange sound escapes from deep within me and I shake my head furiously, trying to shake away that horrible image from my mind.

Someone told me that this would get easier with time, but it never does. It seems to get harder to leave him every time that I do. Everything that I do is a constant reminder that he doesn't get to do it. Everything is a constant reminder of life without Tate, and I can't bear the weight of it. It feels heavier as more time passes. I'm falling deeper and deeper into a dark hole and I have no idea how to get back out. I don't know if I can.

I'm not sure why I spend so much time at the cemetery. When Jase questions me about it, I can't seem to put it into words that make sense to him. I know that the part of Tate that made him Tate isn't in the ground, but it feels easier to connect with him here. It's a place where I can visit him and talk to him that is separate from the rest of life. I don't like to think about him being everywhere and seeing everything I do. I don't really care if people think it's weird. No one dares to say anything to me about it, except for Jase of course. Even when he doesn't say it, I can see the questions in his eyes.

What I don't ever say to Jase is that I am ashamed of everything that happened the night that they took Tate from us. I let him down. I couldn't do anything but watch as they hurt him and ultimately killed him. I felt helpless and weak — two things that I've grown to despise about myself. I thought I was making it up to Tate — and to everyone who lost Tate — by helping the police identify the people who attacked us that night. And we did. I helped identify all four of them, but a few months ago three of them were released as part of a plea bargain to indict the fourth. And the anger that I worked so hard to keep at bay until that point bloomed and exploded inside me the day that we found that out. Now the anger consumes every part of me. I don't know what to do with it all.

A single, lonely tear falls down my cheek and I hurriedly wipe it away, embarrassed even though no one else is around. I am so tired of crying. Every time I think I don't have any more tears left, I manage to surprise myself with more.

As I walk through the cemetery gate, my heart is heavy with the constant ache that reminds me that I wasn't able to save him, and after everything that happened, I wasn't able to make it right. Justice wasn't served. I failed yet again.

I take a few deep breaths, trying to steady the emotions that never seem to be in my control anymore. I rub my eyes with my knuckles trying to clear my vision, but everything looks blurry. I can't tell if it's from tears or the few drinks I've had. I stumble over a few rocks, catching one flip flop within the other and tumble to the ground.

"Dammit!" I yell out into the dark, trying to hoist myself back to my feet.

My hands tighten in small fists at my side and I clench my teeth, trying to subdue the instant rage that surfaces so easily now. I'm breathing heavily as I glance down at my legs. The top of my left foot is scraped and there's a thin line of blood running from both skinned knees. I close my eyes tight as I pull out a few pieces of gravel that are stuck in my left knee.

I ignore the blood and continue to walk back in the direction of the summerhouse. I silently hope the guys aren't home yet because I don't feel like listening to another lecture from Jase, or worse, receive the look that he so often likes to give me now. The look consists of a mix of pity, despair and disappointment. I despise the look more than anything. It makes anger rise in my throat. I can't even say that it's Jase who makes me angry. Jase is one of very few people who has been able to make me happy throughout all of this. I just have a hard time showing it. He's the part of life that is still good and I hold onto it with desperation. But my anger escapes at the strangest times and in ways that make it hard for even me to understand what it is I'm angry about. It pours out of me. Sometimes I imagine it like a black cloud of smoke spilling out of me and poisoning everything I do and everyone around me. I give in to it, because I don't feel like I can control it, or at least that's what I tell myself.

I don't know how to make Jase understand what I'm feeling or thinking, because most of the time I don't understand it myself. Part of me thinks I may be irreparably broken now. I worry that my pieces are a puzzle that Jase wants desperately to put back together, but only I understand that they no longer fit.

I think about the times when I was growing up, when my family would work on a puzzle together. We'd empty the contents of the box onto the dining room table and start by putting a small piece of the puzzle together. For the next few days, every time one of us would walk through the dining room, we'd add another piece that fit. Every once in a while, we'd get to the last piece or pieces, only to realize that they were missing all along. The puzzle would sit there, unfinished and waiting for missing pieces that we'd never find, until someone would get tired of the mess and clean it up.

*I worry that I'm like one of those puzzles. What happens if Jase helps me put the pieces back together, only to find that huge pieces are missing?*

He wants something that no longer exists, and I want him to want me as I am now, missing pieces and all. I know that's a lot to ask, so I don't bring it up. Instead I say nothing. I shut down and crawl inside myself or lash out about things that don't matter. I'm driving him away and I can feel it.

My vision is starting to clear along with my head, as the buzz from the beer I drank throughout the night wears off. My mouth feels like sandpaper and my tongue seems swollen inside it. I glance at my hands and notice they are trembling. The rest of the walk feels longer than it should.

By the time I reach the stone driveway of our summerhouse, all I can think about is getting to the kitchen for another drink. When my mind is clear, that helpless feeling suffocates me, leaving me angry and bitter. I don't want to feel that way, so I drink until I start to feel like I'm the carefree person I used to be before all of this.

There is one lonely truck parked sideways in the stone and I smile to myself realizing that Jesse must be home.

I walk up the three short steps to the front door and jog into the kitchen, heading straight for the fridge. This is the second summer I've spent in this house and I am still amazed at the size of the fridge. I can fit inside of it along with some friends. I know this because Alex and I had to try it one evening after a long night out last summer.

The old summerhouse is down the beach a bit. After Tate died, none of us could bring ourselves to go back to that house, so Ryan's dad (known forever to me as Mr. Gematti no matter how many times he has asked me to call him Scott) rented a strip of luxury bungalows that sit directly on the beach. Past the beach where the sand transitions into grass again is our summerhouse. It has two bedrooms and a family room upstairs, and a large open kitchen and living room downstairs that connects to the back deck. Ryan and I stay at the summerhouse. The rest of the boys share the bungalows, with the exception of Jase, who lives in a house about a mile away that he is renovating with his dad. Most nights, though, Jase stays with me at the summerhouse.

Peeking out the window above the kitchen sink, I can just make out Jesse's silhouette at the edge of our short dock. I see a flame spark and his face is cast in an orange yellow glow for a moment before it's dark again.

I grab a tote bag that is sitting on the counter and empty its contents. A pair of sunglasses, lip gloss, nail polish, and a compact fall across the floor. I shrug, making no attempt to clean it up, and dump two armfuls of cold beer into the tote. Kicking a clear path through the mess, I make my way out to the back deck with the tote slung over my shoulder. As I walk out onto the deck, I listen to the nail polish skitter across the floor and hit the wall.

I close the sliding glass door behind me, but the second I hit the open air the smell of marijuana hits me in the face. Pulling the straps of the tote bag higher on my shoulder, I walk to where Jesse is sitting on the dock, the cans clinking together behind me.

When I'm close enough for Jesse to hear me, he turns his head around slowly and a wide smile spreads across his face. His eyes are barely open, and he leans back to rest his head against the railing of the dock.

"A," he says as he reaches a hand to me. "Come sit with me. Where ya' been?"

I unload the tote bag and as the cans clatter onto the dock, a can rolls in Jesse's direction. He immediately picks it up, opens it and hands it to me before opening another for himself. I finish it in two long swigs and wipe my mouth with the back of my hand. I look at Jesse and catch him staring at me. We connect eyes for a moment and he immediately recognizes the look in mine.

"Cemetery?" he asks, making a motion with his hand for me to sit next to him.

I nod and sit down, resting my head on his shoulder. Jesse never pushes me to talk about anything. There's a way that he looks at me at times that tells me he understands without me having to say a word.

"I just want to forget it all for a little bit," I say to him, sitting up and reaching for another can.

He nods and picks up the pipe and a small Ziploc baggie that was hidden inside his pocket. Packing the pipe tightly, he flips the lighter on quickly and inhales deeply. The same pungent odor fills the air around us. Exhaling slowly, Jesse blows the smoke into my face as I scrunch my nose. I've smoked a few times with him but never enjoyed it. It hurts my lungs; I feel like I want to throw up and the incessant coughing is embarrassing. I'm not sure I've ever been able to inhale enough to even get high.

He takes another hit while I finish another beer. The fuzziness in my head is slowly starting to return which makes me smile. Jesse laughs beside me and nudges me with his arm. He hands me the pipe and uses the lighter for me, knowing my fear of fire. I try to inhale, but my lungs fight me, and I am instantly doubled over coughing. I shake my head at Jesse, but he pushes the pipe forward again.

This time I manage to inhale, hold it, inhale deeper and hold it again. When I feel like my lungs are about to burst, I exhale, coughing a few times as I do. Jesse laughs and I laugh with him.

"Better," he says as I hand it back to him.

He lights up two more times as I drink more beer. I'm beginning to feel lighter than air, as if I'm floating. There's a strange buzzing sensation from my head through my fingertips and a ringing in my ears. My arms and legs begin to tingle, and my shoulders relax. I'm not sure if I am high, but I've forgotten all about the cemetery. I reach for the pipe from Jesse and he raises his eyebrows at me, but hands it over. I take two more long hits and the edges of everything around me become soft and blurred.

My arms and legs now feel light and heavy at the same time. My lips and mouth are dry, so I finish the beer I am drinking, throwing the empty can over my shoulder. My head begins to spin as Jesse puts the Ziploc baggie back into his pocket and grabs for my hand. Holding his hand seems to steady the world, but only for a moment. He lies down with his legs hanging over the edge of the dock and tells me to do the same. I mimic him, but that only makes the spinning worse.

I close my eyes and think about being on a carousel, spinning around and around. A faint smile spreads on my lips and I hear Jesse laugh softly next to me. It makes me giggle, which makes him laugh harder and soon we are both laughing crazily. It feels so good to laugh. I squeeze his hand, which is still clasped around mine.

Before long, I drift into a dream where I'm riding on a painted horse with pink hair — its teeth bared in a wicked grin. The outside world is spinning around me, but I can't seem to find a way to get off the horse even though I want to with everything in me.

# 4 - Jase

I check the door again half expecting her to come walking through it, smiling at me so I forget that I've been so worried for the past few hours. But she doesn't.

I stopped drinking more than an hour ago, wanting to go home, but Ryan convinced me to stay and help Jackson get everyone else home. I gather the guys and tell them it's time to head back. I nod at Jackson, who drew the short straw tonight and is the designated driver. We manage to wrangle our friends into our trucks and head back toward the summerhouse.

I typically sleep in A's room. We made a promise a long time ago to never go to bed angry, so even on days when we are fighting, I usually stay at the summerhouse or she stays with me. I love sleeping next to her, close enough to feel her warmth all night.

Ryan and Ashleigh are in the front row of the truck with me, and Zac and Ace are in the backseat. Jackson's truck is filled with Alex, Mikey and Austin. Ace was finally able to track Jesse down and he apparently went out with some other friends tonight and is already back at the summerhouse.

On the way home, I drive through the cemetery to see if A's still there, but she isn't. A moment of panic fills my chest, but I try to act like I'm not worried. Ryan sees right through it.

"Dude, she's probably home already."

For someone whose younger brother died not too far from here, he doesn't seem to share the panic and worry that I do. Everyone else is silent. They all seem as uncomfortable in the cemetery as I am. I pull back onto the street where it happened, only a few miles in the opposite direction, and head towards home. Well, not my home I guess, but A's home, at least for the summer. And wherever A lives feels like home to me.

Jackson beats me to the house and as we pull into the stone driveway, I can hear the crunch of feet hopping from his truck. I immediately notice Jesse's truck parked sideways in the driveway and shake my head at it.

"He can be such an asshole," I hear Ace's southern slur from the backseat, pointing to his brother's truck.

Ace usually ignores Jesse's antics, hoping that it will one day fix itself. We all worry about Jesse a bit, knowing he parties too much and too often, but A seems to consume me lately and I haven't been able to focus on anything else. Part of me is angry and frustrated with Jesse because he seems to connect with Ayla in a way that I can't.

The rest of the guys have stumbled down the beach into the bungalows, most likely heading to bed. I walk into the kitchen and immediately notice that the fridge is wide open. There are sunglasses and makeup sprawled across the floor. Ashleigh is crouched in the corner of the kitchen near the sliding door to the deck. She picks up a few pieces of what looks like glass or plastic in her hands to show them to Ryan. As I get closer, I notice silver splotches on the floor and the lower part of the wall.

"This was my favorite nail polish," Ashleigh whines as Ryan grabs a broom to sweep up the mess.

I walk over to the fridge and close the door, thinking to myself that maybe Jesse had come home drunk, making a mess as he stumbled through the house. That's when I see her through the kitchen window. She's lying on her back at the end of the dock. I can barely make out her silhouette.

I jog out the back door, ignoring Ryan's voice calling my name in confusion. When I reach her, I realize that Jesse is with her, too. They are both passed out, sprawled awkwardly across the dock. There is a black bag with two full beers inside sitting in between her and Jesse. The rest of the area around them is littered with empty cans. The worry that filled my chest earlier turns to anger now as I realize that she left me alone without telling me where she was going to get drunk with Jesse.

*Awesome.*

I consider leaving them both here until morning, but the idea of A waking up next to someone else makes my stomach churn. I grind my teeth and start to fill the bag with the empty cans as Jesse begins to wake up. He opens one eye, then both and locks eyes with me. I continue picking up the cans as I watch him pull his hand from hers quickly.

"Jase — let me do that," Jesse says, rolling to his side and pushing himself up on unsteady legs.

I ignore him and clean up the last few empty cans around them.

"What happened to her legs, Jesse?" I ask him gruffly when I notice the dried blood smeared from her knees to her ankles.

"What?"

Jesse seems honestly confused as he notices the blood for what seems like the first time.

"I don't know, Jase. I didn't realize … I didn't notice it before."

A takes a sharp breath in, something she does in her sleep often that usually scares the crap out of me. I hand the bag of empty cans to Jesse and he heads off in the direction of the bungalows to sleep off whatever he is currently coming down from.

Shaking my head and mumbling under my breath, I put my arms underneath her and pick her up to carry her inside. She stirs as I lift her and turns her head to face me. When she opens her eyes, I can tell that she is high which only makes me angrier.

"Jase?" she asks as if a question and tries to smile at me, but it doesn't quite reach the corners of her mouth.

I bring her inside, carrying her past Ryan who is still cleaning the kitchen. Ashleigh is nowhere in sight. Ryan takes one look at my face and knows enough not to say a word. He looks at me sadly, but silently moves out of my way as I walk by. I carry her up the stairs and when I reach the top step, she seems to come out of the stupor she was in moments before.

She shakes her head and opens her eyes wider. I walk into the bathroom with her still in my arms and sit her down on the closed toilet seat. She looks at me with a sadness in her eyes that tugs at my heart and I put my head down to hide the sudden emotion threatening at the back of my throat.

When I find my voice, I look up again and she has tears brimming in her eyes. She looks away from me, not wanting me to see her upset. I grab a washcloth, run it under warm water and begin to slowly and carefully clean the dried blood from her legs.

When I look up again, she's looking down at me and we lock eyes for a moment. The tears are gone now, but the sadness is still there. I want to hold her until it goes away, but instead I ask her a simple question.

"What happened?"

Her gaze never drops from mine.

"I fell walking home earlier."

She pauses for a moment, trying to decide what to say next.

"I forgot about it by the time I got home."

She seems embarrassed, knowing that I know it was more than a simple memory lapse. She turns away from me then but continues to talk while looking at the tile instead.

"I'm sorry. You don't need to take care of me."

She reaches a hand down to pull the washcloth from me, but I pull back.

"Let me finish this. Please," I beg her, the anger vanishing immediately because of the vulnerability in her eyes.

I know she hates to have someone dote on her, but she pulls her hand back without a word and lets me continue. Even amidst her lows, she'll let me do something she despises to make me feel better.

I finish cleaning her legs and move to her knees, leaving the brown stained washcloth in the tub next to us. She winces when I clean out the cuts but smiles at me when I look up. She lets me bandage both knees and then carry her to bed.

I tuck her in and turn to leave, planning to head back to my house instead, but she pulls me back to her. She's always pulling me back in.

"Stay. Please," she says, this time begging me.

She says something else, but the pillow muffles her voice. I sigh, thinking that I should leave, but knowing that I won't. I pull back the covers next to her and crawl into bed in my clothes.

I get under the covers and she curls her body into me, falling asleep almost instantly. Her breathing slows and evens out. I lay there for a long time staring at the ceiling because I can't sleep. I can smell the faint aroma of marijuana in her hair mixed with the flowery scent of her shampoo. I pull her tighter to me and she sighs comfortably in her sleep. Kissing the top of her head, I wish that I could keep her here in my arms always but knowing now more than ever that I can't protect her from whatever she is battling, and it scares the hell out of me.

# 5 - Ayla

I open my eyes and stifle a yawn as I listen to Jase snore quietly next to me. My arms and legs feel heavy with sleep even though I've been in bed for the past eight hours. My tongue feels swollen and my mouth is bone dry. There is a slow pounding in my head, but I try to ignore it.

I roll over within Jase's embrace and look at his closed eyes. He looks peaceful, the way he used to look before the lines of worry creased his forehead like they typically do now. I resist the urge to kiss him and wake him up. He doesn't get much sleep lately — mostly because of me.

Instead, I slowly move out of his arms to get out of bed, careful not to wake him. I look down at my bandaged knees and a surge of guilt spreads through me. I look over at Jase again, who hasn't moved, and watch his chest rise and fall as he breathes.

I walk into the bathroom and wipe the sleep from my eyes. My head is still throbbing as I fumble through a drawer under the sink for aspirin. When I find it, I drop two into my mouth and swallow them without water. Glancing in the mirror, I notice large, dark circles under my eyes. I shake my head at my reflection in disappointment and decide to jump in the shower after I finish brushing my teeth.

I remove my clothes and the bandages from my knees, leaving them both on the floor. I get in the shower, pull the curtain around the porcelain tub and turn on the showerhead above me. I move the handle to hot water, even though it's probably close to eighty-five degrees outside already. There's something about a hot shower that makes me feel cleansed — like it's giving me a new start.

I wash my hair as my foot slips on something. Regaining my balance, I look down at the washcloth that Jase used to clean my legs last night. Another surge of guilt spreads through my chest as the voice inside my head reprimands me.

*You're destroying him little by little. You need to stop drinking. Get your life back in control, A. If not for your sake, then for his because he deserves better.*

That little voice inside my head seems to get more and more disgusted with me by the day. I can't say I blame her. I start every day telling myself I won't have a drink today because that seems to make everything worse. Then I tell myself I'll just have one which turns into two which turns into five or six. The alcohol always tricks me into believing I feel better, letting me temporarily forget the things that make me sad or angry or both. When I wake up, I realize everything I'm trying to get away from is right there waiting for me where I left it. What's worse is that I manage to hurt and disappoint everyone around me that I care about, especially Jase.

I reach for the washcloth and try to scrub the blood from it, but the dark orange marks don't fade. Sighing, I drop it back onto the floor of the tub and continue to wash my hair.

I hate that Jase worries about me, but I also resent it, which makes me hate myself even more. I know if the tables were turned, I'd be worried about him, too. I just wish I could go unnoticed for a little while. I hate feeling like my shortcomings are always on display. My head is constantly a mass of confusing thoughts, fleeting pieces of memories, unwavering grief and pent up rage. It makes me feel crazy. Sometimes I simply need to be by myself to get it under control. I know he wants to help me. I would want to help him, too. But there are some things I need to do alone, and I can't seem to get him to understand that without hurting him. And I hate hurting him. Despite that, I lash out at him and run away, tears filling my eyes as I do.

I know that I love Jase. I have never doubted that. He makes me feel things that no one else ever has. He helped me through the worst time in my life. I know that Jase is the best thing that's ever happened to me. I only worry that I may be the worst thing that has happened to him.

I fear he would be better off without me, but I can't imagine my life without him in it. It makes me feel selfish, but I'm not sure if I could survive without him.

Jase is sweet, caring and likes to see the good in people. Jase knows exactly what he wants to be and do with his life, while I have no clue anymore. I'm lost and floundering, and I sometimes worry that he'll wander so far away from what he wants in order to rescue me that neither of us will find our way back again. Jase would give up everything for me, but I don't want him to give up anything for me. He deserves more.

I rinse the last of the conditioner from my hair and let the hot water run over me from the top of my head. There's a soft knock on the door, even though I left it slightly open. I hear Jase clear his throat on the other side of the curtain and I know he's trying to decide what to say.

His silhouette fills the doorway as he says, "Morning."

I turn the water off, smiling to myself. I peek out from behind the curtain, wink at him and gather as much enthusiasm as I can.

"Good morning, babe!"

Jase laughs at my good mood and shakes his head.

"It is, is it?"

"It could be," I say to him with a grin.

I pull the curtain back farther, but Jase is already lifting his shirt over his head, his eyes never leaving mine. I turn the hot water back on as he finishes undressing and gets in the shower with me.

The water runs over us as he pulls me close to him and something unravels inside me. He holds me to him for a few moments and then his mouth finds mine and he kisses me hungrily. My hands rest on the small of his back, pulling his waist closer to mine. He kisses my neck and beneath my ear as my hands move up to the back of his head. He lifts me up in one motion, wrapping my legs around his waist and pushing me against the wall at the back of the tub. His mouth slowly kisses the line of my collarbone as my head falls back. I close my eyes and enjoy the moment. This morning, I let Jase be my drug, letting everything else slip from my mind.

I wish it could always be like this when I'm with Jase. I wish I could just forget all of it and be the same person he fell in love with. I selfishly cling to him as his mouth finds mine again, hoping that Jase doesn't realize what I already know — that person doesn't exist anymore.

# 6 - Ayla

I hide my fingers underneath me as I sit at the table in the kitchen eating a bowl of fruit. They look like little raisins, wrinkly and pale from all the time spent in the shower this morning. A faint smile spreads across my face as I think about it.

"Someone is in a good mood this morning," Ryan says to me with a grin as he sits down across from me.

He looks in my eyes, winks once and reaches across the table to grab my hand. He squeezes it briefly.

"You good, Sunshine?"

Sunshine was Tate's nickname for me, and since his death, Ryan is the only person I let call me that. He only uses it when he's worried about me, but he never seems to judge me even when I think he probably should.

"Yeah. I'm trying to be," I say, squeezing his hand in return.

Ryan nods at me slowly with a smile weighed down with his own grief.

"That's all you can do, A. That's all we can try to do."

He pauses for a moment, and when he looks back up at me, his electrifying smile has returned. It always amazes me how quickly he can turn it on like that. I wish he could teach me how to do the same.

"So, was it a good night, a good morning, or both?" he asks, moving his eyebrows up and down.

I laugh, shaking my head, and playfully push him on the shoulder.

"It was a great morning," Jase says as he walks into the kitchen, his hair still damp.

I blush the color of the watermelon sitting in front of me as he walks behind me and kisses my cheek. He winks at me when he sits down next to me, his hand finding mine and pulling it into his lap. He takes my fork and stabs at the watermelon left in my bowl, knowing that I won't eat it.

The three of us sit at the table for a while, laughing and eating, as they fill me in on what I missed last night. Ryan tells me about Austin doing the worm across the dance floor and the three of us erupt in laughter. Austin, who is so very quiet, loves to dance even though he has the most obscure dance moves. When we're out at night, it's not odd for him to break out the "shopping cart," the "typewriter," the "lawnmower," or my personal favorite, the "sprinkler."

Our laughing stops abruptly when Ashleigh stalks into the room and slams her tiny fist on the table in front of me. I look up at her in surprised confusion. Ryan begins to stand up, putting his arms up in front of her.

"Ash–" he starts, but she pushes his arms aside interrupting him.

"Don't 'Ash' me," she says to Ryan. "I'm so tired of you defending her all the time. I'm your girlfriend, Ryan. You should stand up for me, but no, you're out here laughing it up like I don't even exist."

I notice the way Ryan flinches when she uses the word girlfriend. Normally, he would have corrected her, since he still claims they are just friends, but this time his mouth remains closed in a tight line.

Ashleigh turns to look at me, her eyes fierce with anger.

"I don't know what the hell your problem is, but it's time you get your shit together, A."

My confusion quickly turns to anger. I grit my teeth, trying to keep it at bay. I can feel my pulse in my neck and fingers. Jase squeezes my hand and I try to calm myself before I find my voice. It scares me how quick that anger can come, but Ryan speaks before my words can surface.

"Ash, it was just some makeup and nail polish. Relax. I'll get you more."

Ryan puts his hand over her fist on the table and tries to pull her to a seat next to him. She yanks her hand from underneath his.

"Unbelievable!" she yells at him, jabbing her finger in the air at him. "You are unbelievable. How long are you going to make excuses for her? You let whatever guilt you're carrying over your brother cloud your friendship with her."

She venomously spits the word friendship as if it leaves a bad taste in her mouth.

"She needs to grow up!"

Ryan opens his mouth to speak but is shocked into silence. No words come. The entire room is silent. I've known Ashleigh for four years now and I've never seen her talk to him like that. She turns back to me, this time pointing her finger in my face.

"It's been two years, so get over it already. Everyone lost him, A. Not just you. He was Ryan's brother, for crying out loud, and you don't see him acting the way you do. Stop begging for attention. I felt sorry for you in the beginning, but now it's just pathetic. You're pathetic."

She finishes the second pathetic by stabbing her finger into my left shoulder. I see red at the corners of my vision and every ounce of logic has left my mind. I am out of my seat and shoving her before I know what I'm doing. She stumbles backwards and almost falls, but Ryan catches her at the last moment. Luckily, Jase grabs both of my arms from behind me with his, yanking and pushing me out the back door of the kitchen.

He guides me off the deck and into the grass and pushes me to a seated position. The adrenaline coursing through me causes my hands to shake uncontrollably, so I put them underneath me again.

"A, what the hell?!" Jase says to me in a rough voice, full of anger of his own.

There's a fire burning in my eyes as I snap my head up and stare into his face.

"What the hell?!" I throw back at him. "I guess I should have sat there and let Ashleigh talk to me like that — like I'm a child?"

Jase interrupts me before I can continue.

"Maybe because you act like a child sometimes."

He tilts his head at me, the way he usually does when he's trying to make a point. No words come to mind because my temper has taken up every space in my head. I pull away from Jase and stalk towards the dock, eager to get away from him. He catches up to me quickly, grabbing for my hand, but I yank it away, spinning to face him.

"A, wait. Don't walk away! Talk to me. Ashleigh is pissed about last night."

I shake my head, Jase's words not making any sense. I didn't see or talk to Ashleigh last night. I left the bar to head to the cemetery before she even got there.

"What are you talking about?" I say to him, more harshly than I mean to.

"A, you dumped her bag and filled it with beer. We came home to her stuff all across the kitchen and her nail polish was shattered on the floor."

He grabs for my hand again and this time I let him take it. That quickly, the anger is gone, and in its place is shame and guilt. A memory of me kicking the nail polish on the way out of the door last night comes to mind and quickly fades like fog dispersing.

*How did I not remember that?*

I keep losing huge chunks of time.

"Oh," is all I say, even though my mind is filling with various forms of apologies.

"You didn't remember."

Jase doesn't ask it as a question, but simply makes the statement. He doesn't do anything to hide the disappointment in his voice. I sink to my knees, not wanting to meet Jase's eyes. Jase crouches next to me, his hands squeezing both of my arms steadying me. He kisses my forehead and I crumple under the weight of my own self-hate. He sits down on the grass and pulls me into his lap. I curl into him and rest my head underneath his chin. We sit like this in silence for a few minutes.

I try to remember coming home last night or why I had dumped her stuff on the floor to begin with. I have no answers. I think I simply didn't care at the time. I don't even recognize myself anymore. I let a wave of self-pity wash over me.

"Why do you stay with me?" I say out loud before I can think better of it.

"What?" Jase says, surprised by my question.

He pulls my chin up with his hand, so I look into his face.

"How could you even ask that? I love you!"

"Yeah, but maybe you'd be better off without me."

I'm fearful that it's true as the words leave my tongue. Jase rolls his eyes at me, frustrated once again.

"Why do you push me away when you're mad at yourself? I'll never understand it. Let me in, A. I can help you. Please, let me help you."

Jase's voice rises and he is pleading with me once again. I hear the desperation in his voice. I know he wants to help me any way that he can. I want to turn back into his embrace and tell him that I love him, too. I want to cry the tears that I keep buried inside me until there are none left to poison me with. I want to let him help me because I think I need help, but don't know how to be okay with asking for it. I want to open up to him, but I can't. So instead, I get up abruptly and walk down the beach alone, ignoring Jase's voice calling my name from where he still stands.

# 7 - Jase

I watch her disappear down the beach, unsure of whether I should follow her or not. Every instinct is telling me to, but I don't have the energy for another fight. I'm not even sure that she's mad at me, but who knows anymore?

I run both hands through my hair and interlock my fingers behind my head. I stare out over the water and watch as the sun dances off the surface. It reminds me of our shower this morning and I want to rewind time. How did the morning start so perfectly and yet, we still ended up here — in a fight and her disappearing like she always does? I wish she would stop running away from me. I'm starting to get really tired of it.

I hear the screen door open and close behind me, and I turn around to see Ryan on the back deck with Ashleigh close behind him. She sheepishly peeks around him at me.

Ryan has been my best friend for as long as I can remember, and Ashleigh has been following him around for almost as long. I don't think we'll ever be great friends, but I have spent a lot of time with her over the years because of Ryan. I think she means more to him than he lets on. I'll never fully understand their relationship, if that's what you want to call it, but when Ayla spends her summers with us, Ashleigh is attached to Ryan's hip.

"Sorry about that, Jase," Ashleigh says to me as she looks down at her feet.

I shrug at both of them and try to smile, knowing that Ashleigh has a right to be angry. I would have handled it differently, but Ashleigh isn't known for her grace or empathy.

"Where's A now?" Ryan asks me, taking a step off the deck and putting a hand on my shoulder.

I nod in the direction down the beach that A is heading. We can make out her figure in the distance, walking at a steady pace away from us. Ryan looks as sad as I feel as he watches her. He continues staring, even after we can no longer see her, and squeezes my shoulder.

"She's working it out the best way she knows how. Let her do her thing. She'll make some mistakes and we'll be there for her every time she does. That's how we help her."

I'm not so sure he's right, but I don't say so.

"Seriously, Ryan?" Ashleigh says, anger filling her voice again as she narrows her eyes at him and puts her hands on her hips.

"What?" Ryan says to her with a shrug but looks at me with a grin.

I hear footsteps behind us, and we turn to see Alex, Jackson and Zac walking up the small hill from the bungalows.

"Wanna take the boats out?" Alex asks when they are a little closer.

"Yeah, we should all go," Zac adds, pounding Alex a little too hard on the back based on the way he flinches.

"Where's A?" Jackson asks immediately, looking from my face to Ryan's and back again.

Before I can answer, Ashleigh jumps into the conversation from the deck.

"She went for a walk down the beach."

"I'll stay behind and wait for her," I hear myself saying before I even think it, but Zac shakes his head.

"No way, Jase. You're coming with us. We'll stay close in case A comes back. Besides, I need someone who knows what they're doing on a wakeboard because these idiots have no clue," Zac says, pointing over his shoulder at Alex and Jackson.

I think to myself that A's pretty damn good on a wakeboard, but I pound Zac's fist and start walking toward the dock anyway. I hate the thought of leaving her behind, but that seems to be what she wants lately.

An hour later, despite the fact that A is still at the back of my mind, I'm laughing and having a good time. Zac and I finish our turns on the boards while Ryan drives the boat. Alex and Jackson try after us, but neither of them is able to get more than a few minutes upright. Austin and Mikey go next and they don't do much better. Before long, we are laughing at them as they try to untangle from each other's lines.

Zac sits down next to me and offers me a cold bottle of water. We both drink in silence for a few minutes, staring out at the water as the rest of the guys try to untie the knots that are now in the ropes.

"Hey, man, you okay?" Zac asks before he finishes the rest of his water.

I shake my head slowly.

"Not really. I mean, I guess I am. But I don't know what to do about A anymore. I don't think she's okay, but she won't talk to me about it."

Zac nods for a moment before he responds.

"Yeah, I know what you mean. I've tried to talk to her a few times about … it … but she always manages to smile and tell me she's fine. I can understand that she doesn't want to relive it all. Who would?"

He stops and reaches into the cooler for another bottle of water. We're both silent for another minute before he continues.

"I guess I just want to make sure you know we're all in this together. Ayla is just as much a part of us as you, me or Ryan. We all care about her. You don't have to carry anything alone, Jase. You've got eight brothers standing with you."

I don't have a chance to say anything in response because Alex calls for Zac to help him with the knotted ropes in front of him. Zac gets up and walks to the back of the boat, but I don't move from my spot. I finish what's left of my water and reach for another, trying to swallow the newly formed lump in my throat.

Even though Mikey is the oldest of all of us, Zac has always been the one to keep an eye out for everyone else. He's an only child, and his parents traveled often when we were growing up, leaving him alone even before he was old enough to really fend for himself. Our group has always been his family in a lot of ways, so it's important to him that we all take care of each other. Even knowing all of this, Zac's words take me by surprise. I sometimes forget that we are all going through this together.

*Maybe A forgets that, too.*

I pick my head up and catch Jesse staring at me. He immediately looks away and plays with the plastic cup in his hand. I get up and walk over to where he is sitting. He looks at me like he wants to say something but looks at his feet instead.

"How's everything, Jesse?" I ask him as I sit down next to him.

He looks at me wide-eyed before he responds.

"Good, Jase. I mean, uh, yeah, everything is good."

He fumbles with the cup before putting it next to him.

"About last night … nothing happened, you know? I was all kinds of messed up. I remember A coming down to the dock. I thought she was going to give me a hard time about it, but she sat down and offered me a beer instead. I was glad to have the company."

Jesse trails off, looking slightly embarrassed.

I've never been very close with Jesse, but he's been tagging along with Ace since we were kids. Jesse and Tate migrated into our group of friends because of Ace and Ryan, and it wasn't until Tate moved up to high school that we stopped referring to them as the "kid brothers."

Before Ayla came along, Tate and Jesse were inseparable for a while, but Tate was a year younger than Jesse and two grades below the rest of us. In high school, Jesse and Tate grew apart a bit, falling in with different crowds. There was never any bad blood between them, but Tate got left behind quite a bit and he was constantly frustrated because we let Jesse tag along when he couldn't. It wasn't an issue as much when Ayla started spending summers with us because Tate had a friend to be left behind with.

If I had to guess, I think Jesse feels guilty about leaving Tate behind, but we all carry guilt for something when it comes to Tate. In some ways, we all let Tate down before the night he was killed. And we all have to find a way to deal with that. As my father would say, we need to act like men because that's what we are now. I get frustrated easily with Jesse because he doesn't seem to be able to do that, and for some reason, this creates a bond between him and A. I wonder sometimes if I would be more sympathetic with Jesse if he and Ayla weren't as close. I turn to him as I consider this.

"I think A was pretty messed up last night, too. You both seem to be doing your own thing lately, and none of us know what's going on with either one of you."

Jesse looks angry, but only for a second, and then I worry that he is going to cry instead. I wouldn't know what to do or say if he started crying right now, but thankfully he doesn't. He swallows loudly as he gulps down whatever is left in his plastic cup.

"Don't worry about me. I'm good—"

*Yeah right.*

"—and A will be, too. She just needs to work out some crap or whatever."

I sigh, frustrated, and sit back farther in the bench seat.

"Yeah, Ryan said the same thing earlier. I don't know how to help her work through it, Jesse. You seem to understand what she's going through better than I do. How do I help her?"

Jesse laughs sarcastically.

"She only feels more comfortable talking to me because I'm as screwed up as she is—"

He stops abruptly, seemingly embarrassed for saying so out loud.

"I didn't mean that she's screwed up ... "

He looks at his feet as he throws the empty cup into the plastic bag that hangs next to him.

"I think we're all a little screwed up now, especially A. I hate that she's sad all the time when she used to be so happy. And of course, she's sad. She should be. We all are. I just hate that I can't make it better for her. I want to. I really, really want to and I know that I can't. Sometimes, though, it seems like you can, even if it's just for a short time, and it feels like she doesn't want me to even try."

I stop talking as Jesse shakes his head, frustrated with me, like I'm not understanding some secret that I should. He opens his mouth, changes his mind and gets up instead without saying anything. He's takes a few awkward steps away from me toward the front of the boat before he stops to look back at me.

"The best thing you can do is stop treating her like there's something wrong with her that needs to be fixed. Just be there for her like you always are and when she's ready, she'll talk about it. It may take longer than you'd like, but she'll open up to you eventually."

He must see the frustration in my face, and it echoes in his own. He takes a step toward me with his eyes squinted, suddenly angry although I'm unsure why.

"She really loves you, you know? This isn't about you. This is about her trying to figure out how to live with it."

He spits out the words as he glances around and lowers his voice to just above a whisper.

"Remember how angry you felt that night?! When we all realized what they'd done to Tate — that he was gone, that they kicked the shit out of Ayla and made her watch? Can you imagine what that must have been like for her? To watch something like that happen to someone you love? Ayla is protective of all of us, but you remember how fierce she was about standing up for Tate. Those pieces of shit made her feel helpless and she has to live with that for the rest of her life. She has to live with the fact that she was the only one there and couldn't do anything to stop it. Do you have any idea how that must make her feel? I hate that we weren't there when it happened, not just for Tate, but for her, too! I get so damn angry thinking about it, and then to find out that three of them are getting away with it?! I don't have a clue what she goes through, Jase, but I know how I feel about it. I'm not sure how to help her either, but I think you're right. I think we all are a little screwed up now. I think we all need to work through how to live with everything that's happened. Some of you guys deal with it better than we do. Maybe A and I are just more honest with ourselves about how we feel than everyone else. Maybe you guys are better at forgetting than we are. Maybe we need help to forget."

That's the most I've heard Jesse say in a long time, maybe ever. He drops his eyes and uncurls his fists. He wipes his mouth with the back of his hand and slumps back into the seat across from me. I can't help but to feel more frustrated with him than usual.

"You may be right about a lot of things, Jesse, but I don't see how drowning your sorrows in alcohol or drugs solves anything. That's not being honest. You're just running away from things you don't want to deal with. It's never going to get better that way. In some ways, it'll only get worse."

Memories flash through my mind from growing up, but Jesse's laugh quickly brings me back to the present. He waves an arm across the boat towards the garbage bag full of empty cans, plastic cups and bottles.

"We're all running away from shit, Jase. If she needs to be on her own, or sit at the cemetery, or drink to get away from all of it for a bit, then she should. Who are we to judge?"

Before I can respond, he gets up and walks into the cabin with his head hung low. I stare out at the water long after Jesse leaves, letting everything he said sink in, my heart sinking with it.

# 8 - Ayla

A trickle of sweat slides down my back between my shoulder blades.

*It's so damn hot.*

I would pick the hottest part of the day to trek down the beach and into town. I look down at the plastic bag in my hand and pull a bottle of iced tea from it. I silently wish it were a beer and then get mad at myself for thinking it. Drinking seems to get me into trouble with — well — everyone lately.

The iced tea is already starting to warm, even though I only bought it ten minutes ago. The plastic bottle is covered in a film of condensation and it almost slips from my fingers.

I contemplate walking in the direction of the cemetery, but then think of Jase, and decide to head back toward the house instead. I feel horrible about leaving him on the beach earlier and wish I knew how to express what I'm feeling better than I do. I'm sure to Jase it seems like I don't care, but that couldn't be further from the truth.

On the way home, I think about the things I want to say to Jase. I don't know why it has always been difficult for me to tell someone I care about them. I have always tried to show it in my actions because saying it out loud makes me feel like I'm giving a piece of myself away. With Jase, it's different. I'd give every piece of me that I have to Jase, but somehow everything I feel now — love, hate, anger, joy, despair, guilt — it's all tied up together, and I can never seem to pull only one out by itself.

Last year, spending the first summer in Virginia without Tate was more difficult than I ever imagined it would be. Going to all of the same places that I went with Tate just reminded me that he wasn't with us. There was an obvious hole no matter what I did or where I went. Almost every memory I made here had Tate in it somehow. Jase started taking me exploring to find places I had never been before, to make new memories with him that didn't feel empty or like something was missing. He took me to new islands, and we found a waterfall and a bunch of caves. He brought me to restaurants just outside of town or to historic sites and museums that I'd never been to before. The rest of the guys started joining us and they took turns coming up with new places that we could visit or explore together as a group.

I smile to myself as the memories come to mind. We all came together last summer, closer than ever before. Now some of us are unraveling at the seams.

*Becauese they're getting away with it.*

My mind screams at me as I grind my teeth and grip the iced tea bottle in my hand so tightly that my fingers turn white. I take a few deep breaths, trying to calm down my racing heart. And then it comes flooding back, like it usually does, all at once.

*I call out his name and he turns to walk toward me, but that's when I notice the black Jeep approaching.*

*The egg hits the front of my dress as they yell, "Fag Hag!"*

*I want Tate to run away, but I can't seem to get the words out. The Jeep pulls over and three figures jump out wearing masks from the gala.*

I flinch, trying to stop the memory, but once it starts to play in my head, it's impossible to.

*I struggle with all my might, even though one of them is holding me down, holding my head so I have to watch. They continue to punch and kick Tate, the sound of their blows echoing in my ears.*

*They scream at him, even though Tate is no longer conscious. I hear a crunching sound that I will never forget as they kick Tate in the face one final time and his body sags.*

*The commotion that follows as people form a crowd on the side of the road while I hold Tate in my arms as he takes his last breath …*

*The sound of sirens in the distance …*

*Watching Mr. Gematti crumple when he sees Tate …*

*The detective trying to ask me questions …*

*It all swirls together in a nonsensical way, confusing and terrifying me.*

*I stare into the blinking red light of the camera at the police station, the light that takes me immediately back to the gala where it all started.*

*I stand behind a pane of glass in the police station, identifying all four of them from a lineup, fulfilling my promise to Mr. Gematti that we'd make them pay.*

I absent-mindedly wipe tears from my eyes as I continue on my walk, sipping the now warm tea, as I remember the day I found out they weren't going to pay after all.

*I am sitting in class when my phone goes off. Embarrassed that I forgot to turn off the ringer, I blush crimson and silence it quickly. The professor glares at me from the front of the room and I mutter an almost inaudible apology. I don't even look at who was calling. By the time the class ends I have 12 missed calls. Panic rises from my stomach and spreads through my arms and legs like lead as I scroll through the call log. They are all from Jase, Ryan and my father. I call dad first, bracing myself for bad news. I am almost in tears by the time he picks up the phone.*

*"Dad? What is it? What's going on?"*

*"Ayla, where are you?"*

*Dad's voice sounds alarmingly unsteady.*

*"I'm leaving class. I'm on my way home. What's going on? Is everyone okay?"*

*I try to hide the fact that I'm crying but fail miserably.*

*"Come straight home. Everyone is okay, but I have some news about the trial."*

*I take a deep breath in relief. Everyone is okay. Everyone is safe. I repeat this as a mantra for the quick ride home.*

*When I walk into the living room, my mother is in tears. Dad gets up and walks me to the couch to sit down before sitting down himself. He tells me that he received a phone call from Detective Van Wagner while I was in class and that three of the four people who attacked me and murdered Tate were being released from jail. It is part of some kind of plea bargain. Dad tells me in detail what this means, but I am already somewhere far away and no longer listening. All I can think about is the promise I made to Mr. Gematti and Ryan; that we would find the people who did this to Tate and make them pay. I feel failure sit heavy in my stomach.*

*When dad finishes talking, I go to my room and crawl in bed even though it is still daylight out. Mom and dad both check on me, but I smile at them weakly, trying harder to comfort them than myself. I don't think I have any sadness left in me. Anger and fear fill the empty spaces the sadness leaves behind. I'm not afraid of the three of them coming after me again. I'm afraid of what I'll do if they try.*

*I talk to Ryan and Jase on the phone later that night. They are with the rest of the guys, but I ask them not to put me on speakerphone like they usually do. I can hear them talking over one another in the background, angry voices rising above each other. Ryan and I don't say much, but I can tell by the sound of his voice that he feels completely defeated. He says that his dad is flipping out and calling all of his lawyers, but that there's not much they can do at this point. I nod silently, as if Ryan can see me. He tells me not to worry because they are filing restraining orders on all three of them. There is more awkward silence and then Ryan hands the phone to Jase.*

*"Hi," I say in a small voice that doesn't sound like my own.*

*"Hi. I want to ask if you're okay, but of course you're not. None of us are. Do you want me to come visit?"*

*I am nodding my head furiously as I squeeze my comforter between my fingers but tell him no out loud. I start building the foundation to the wall around how I feel about all of this.*

*"I'm okay, Jase, really."*

*I build another layer on top of the foundation.*

*"I'm frustrated by it, of course, but I'm fine."*

*The wall is chest height now, but I keep building because I don't want to admit that I once again feel helpless, just like I did the night that Tate died. Jase's voice sounds hurt on the other end of the phone, but the wall keeps going higher and higher anyway.*

*"Okay, babe. I thought you might want company. If you need me, I can be there in eight hours."*

*I let a few silent tears fall, careful to hide them from my voice.*

*"I know. Thank you, but mom and dad are here if I need to talk."*

*I can hear how cutting the words sound, but they tumble out of my mouth before I can stop them. I don't want to be the little bird with the broken wing anymore.*

*"I'll see you next month when I'm back in town. Love ya."*

*Short, disconnected and cold — that's how I sound right now and to Jase of all people. Jase is quiet for a moment, and all I can hear is the background chatter.*

*"Love ya too, A," he says, sounding hurt and confused.*

*I hang up the phone feeling guilty before anyone else can get on the line to speak with me and crawl under the covers.*

I blink a few times, trying to wipe the memory from my mind. I often wonder if the tables were turned, would I have the same amount of patience for Jase that he has had with me. I walk up the driveway to our house, swinging the plastic bag alongside of me and finish the last sip in the bottle as I consider this. He never seems to give up on me, even though I'm positive that he should.

I can hear laughter coming from the back of the house as I head in that direction. When I reach the back deck, all of the guys are sitting around the large, round picnic table Jase built for us last summer. I pause as I realize that Ashleigh is sitting on Ryan's lap and my stomach flips.

*Better get this over with.*

# 9 - Jase

I notice her before anyone else does.

*I always do.*

She walks around the side of the house with a white plastic bag that bounces alongside her with each step. The sun catches her face, reflecting light in her dark eyes and highlighting the faint freckles that run across her nose and cheeks. I watch as she scans all of us gathered around the table playing cards and her gaze stops at Ashleigh. She looks nervous for a quick moment and I have to fight the urge to jump up and walk over to her, knowing that's the last thing she'd want me to do.

She pauses for a moment and then continues on her way toward us. When she hits the bottom step of the deck, Alex yells, "Rocky!" and A breaks out that smile — the one that I wish she wore more. Seeing it light up her face makes me realize how much I truly miss seeing her happy. Alex has playfully called her Rocky since her first summer here, in honor of her surprising, but short-lived temper. Everyone else greets her with fist bumps and hugs. She catches my eye and winks at me, grabbing for my hand and squeezing it to let me know that whatever had gone on earlier is forgotten and we are okay again. I smile and squeeze back before she looks over at Ashleigh.

Of course, Ashleigh has been complaining about her nail polish all afternoon, so by now, everyone knows what happened last night. A clears her throat, and Alex and Zac exchange grins waiting for a heated conversation to erupt. While all of us love having Ayla around, no one has ever been too fond of Ashleigh's presence. So even though she was in the wrong last night, it doesn't stop the guys from silently cheering Ayla on.

Ashleigh looks up, but A doesn't say anything right away. She continues to stare Ashleigh down and I'm having trouble reading her expression. Her face is blank.

"What?!" Ashleigh angrily exclaims when she can't take the silent stare from A anymore.

A doesn't respond but reaches a hand inside the white plastic bag and places a bottle of silver nail polish, identical to the one that she broke last night, in front of Ashleigh. Ashleigh looks down at it and blinks, surprised. I can't contain my smile and I reach a hand up and place it on the small of A's back.

"I had to go to three different stores to find it. I also tried to get a 'Sorry that I was a jerk last night' card, but they seemed to be all out."

Ryan laughs out loud, but Ashleigh still has yet to crack a smile. She reaches out her hand and picks up the nail polish to inspect it.

"Thanks, I guess. I mean, you didn't have to break it in the first place, but whatever. I just hope it doesn't happen again."

Ashleigh squints her eyes at A. I tense up, waiting for A to get angry or fire a nasty response back, but she doesn't. She only looks at Ashleigh and smiles.

"Well, I don't want to make any promises that I can't keep."

A empties the rest of the contents of the white plastic bag onto the table and bottle after bottle of the same nail polish rolls out. There must be at least ten bottles of silver nail polish on the table now.

"Now you have a few extras — just in case."

A raises her eyebrows as Ashleigh laughs out loud before she can think better of it. The rest of us laugh, too, and A sinks into my lap. I wrap my arms around her and breathe in her perfume. She places her arms around mine and rests her hands on top of my own. She squeezes them and leans back into me. Something about her seems lighter today and I realize that her eyes are clear.

"You need a drink, A?" Jesse asks from across the table.

I immediately want to throw something at him. To my surprise, A shakes her head at him.

"I'm good for now."

Jesse's eyes connect with mine for a moment, his face mirroring my surprise. I pull her tighter to me and kiss the side of her face. I'm grateful that she somehow found some peace today, but sad that she seemed to find it by spending time away from me. She leans into my kiss and then moves to sit alongside me at the table. I feel the loss of her from my arms immediately and fight the urge to pull her back into my lap.

"Okay, boys," she says with a wide grin, looking around the table. "Who's ready to lose a few hands of poker?"

# 10 - Jase

When everyone else heads out to eat dinner, Ayla and I stay behind. She rides with me to my renovation house and we walk hand in hand through the field of wildflowers behind the house. She's told me many times that this is one of her favorite places to be, but we haven't spent much time here this year.

We walk in silence for a while and I glance over at her as she reaches her open hand out through the flowers as we walk. Her eyes are closed and something about her expression makes me smile. Her eyes flutter open and she catches me staring at her. She stops abruptly and pulls me to her with her hand covered by mine. She leans in and kisses me lightly, just barely touching my lips. I want more, so I lean forward, but she pulls back playfully. She pauses, and then leans in slowly again, stopping just before her lips touch mine. The corners of her mouth are curled into a grin and I feel my mouth shadowing the movement. I play along, lightly brushing my lips with hers, but I don't have the willpower she does. I move closer and kiss her, achingly slow, and this time she doesn't pull back. I kiss her this way while I pick her up and cradle her in my arms. I don't stop kissing her all the way back to the house and up the stairs to my bedroom.

The sun shines through the bedroom window as it sets, and it highlights the auburn in her dark hair. There's a sparkle in her brown eyes tonight that I haven't seen in a long time and I realize how much I've missed it. She rolls on her side to face me and rests her face on her hand. I'm lying on my back with my hands behind my head because if I didn't keep them there, they would be all over her. She leans down and kisses my forehead, my cheek, just below my lips, and my neck. I close my eyes when I feel her lips on my shoulder and then my chest. When I can no longer take it, my hands move to the sides of her face and lightly pull her face back to mine. I can feel her long eyelashes against my skin as we kiss.

We lay together in my bed for hours talking, touching, laughing and kissing. This is how it used to be for us all the time. This is how I wish we could be again.

I live for these little moments where the outside world drops away and it's only the two of us.

It's dark outside now and the moon shining through the window is our only source of light. She smiles at me and places her hand on my chest. She looks at me intently but pauses as if she's unsure of whether she wants to say what she is about to. I put my hand on top of hers and her features relax.

"I'm sorry I walked away from you this morning. There are so many things that I want to say, and I never seem to get it right because my feelings get tangled up in each other."

I lean in and kiss her softly.

"It's okay. Part of it is my fault, too. I have had a hard time accepting that it's difficult for you to talk to me about certain things because I want to be the person you can talk to about anything. I thought I was until the past few months. And I understand there are things that have happened that you may never be ready to talk about, but I'm here if you ever want to. What I don't understand is why things are so different between you and I now when last summer we were closer than ever?"

I look at her expectantly and she casts her eyes down to our hands. She runs her fingers across the tops of mine, not answering the question.

"A," I say to her, trying to get her to look at me. "Will you please tell me what you're thinking? Are you afraid it will hurt me?"

I sit up, pulling my hands from under her touch as I do. Her bottom lip trembles slightly as she meets my eyes and I feel my stomach drop.

"I don't know how to answer that, Jase. I don't ever want to hurt you, but I seem to do it over and over again. I worry that I'm ruining us. I worry that I'm messed up inside and I'm going to mess you up, too. I worry that I'm spinning out of control, but I don't want you to help me because I want to learn how to help myself. I worry that I'm not the same person I was before … "

She pauses for a moment again, taking a deep breath in.

"I worry that if I say the wrong thing or open up when I'm at my lowest, you won't love me anymore because most of the time I don't love me."

I don't say anything at first but shake my head slowly as she looks at me. I run my thumb along the side of her face.

"That's not possible," I whisper to her softly.

"Jase, there are times when you look at me and I could explode into a million pieces or melt into a puddle right on the spot because I can literally feel the weight of how much you love me. Your love for me is a physical force and it wipes out everything else going on in my head and heart. It takes up space in the room with us. It wraps around me and makes me feel safe even after everything that happened to us. I love when you look at me like that and I want you to keep looking at me like that forever. But the truth is, I don't love myself all the time anymore. I feel different and broken, but I don't want to talk to you about it because I'm worried that you'll start to see me the same way. I'm worried that I'm going to let you in on the secret and you're going to start looking at me the way I see myself. And if that happens, it's all over, Jase. I don't know if I could come back from that."

She pulls herself closer to me and rests her head on my chest. I can't imagine her doing or saying anything that would make me think of her any differently than I do. I try to think back to before I knew I loved her, which was a very long time before I told her that I did.

*I am tearing apart the old kitchen, anxious to get started on the renovation because I know that what I have in mind for the kitchen is going to be one of the longest projects in the whole house.*

*The rest of the guys all went to a party, Alex and Zac ragging on me for not joining them as I left to head here. I drive by A and Tate walking by themselves on the side of the road as I pull out of the Gematti's driveway. I smile and wave as I pass them, thinking about finding A on the side of the road walking home alone from the gala the other night. I had pulled over right away once I realized it was her and hopped out of my truck. When she turned around, she looked so sad and had tears in her eyes. It surprised me because I am used to always seeing her smile. I could tell she didn't want to talk about it. When we got into the truck together, I pulled her into the middle of the bench seat, against my better judgment, so she was closer to me. Back at the after party, she seemed to return to her happy self, but I could still see something bothering her just under the surface. I wanted to reach out and tell her whatever it was would be okay, but I didn't. I stopped by the Gematti's house the next day and took her for pizza. It was the first time I had ever been alone with her, besides the short ride in my truck, and I was surprised at how easy it was to talk to her one on one. Her smile had returned, and I kept fighting the urge to reach out and touch her. Then Ryan and Tate showed up and our time alone ended that quickly.*

*I shake my head as I use a crowbar to tear out another cabinet. I haven't been able to get her out of my head the past few days. I thought Ryan had a thing for her at first, but Ashleigh won't let him out of her sight when A is around. Tate hit it off with her right away, and I think he wants to be more than just friends with her. Who am I to get in the way of that? Ryan is my best friend and Tate is basically my little brother. But no matter how hard I try, I can't ignore the way I feel when I'm around her.*

*I take off my shirt and throw it in the corner. I lift the baseball hat I'm wearing and wipe sweat off my forehead with the back of my hand. The sun is down, but it's still so damn hot. I'm just about to start on another cabinet when I hear footsteps on the front porch. There was some vandalism at the house before dad and I rebuilt the porch and I don't want anyone to destroy anything else. I jog to the front door, turn on the porch light and open it.*

*And there she is.*

*Her arm is raised as if she is about to knock and she jumps about a foot in the air as I open the door. My breath catches for a moment as I stare at Ayla, alone, on my front porch.*

*I flip off the switch and pull her inside, realizing I blinded her with the sudden light. She looks at me, suddenly embarrassed, and all I want to do is kiss her. I shake my head knowing that I shouldn't. I lead her into the kitchen instead, offering her a drink as I put my shirt back on. We end up on the swing on the front porch and I find myself wishing we could sit here all night. I realize then, as I stare at her smile and watch the light reflect in her eyes, that I want to be more than friends with her, too. I reach for her hand and when she lets me take it, I want more. Instead I give her a tour of the house. Usually everyone's eyes glaze over when I talk about the renovations and I sometimes forget that not everyone is as excited about the project as I am. But I can see my excitement dance in her eyes as we walk through the house and I wish I could find more to show her, so I don't have to let her hand go.*

*She offers to help me with the work in the kitchen and I laugh at her. I can't imagine little A tearing apart cabinets, but she insists, and I don't want her to leave so I agree.*

I'll never forget that night, and even though I didn't kiss her for another two years after that, I'll always silently consider that our first date.

The renovation house is something that dad and I dreamed up when I was a kid. He helped me save up for it and helped with a down payment once we found the perfect house. It's been four years since that first night with A. There is still so much to be done on the house, but A has helped me every summer since.

*Dad joins us often and the three of us work on the house into morning. One night, after she leaves, dad says to me, "You realize you have to marry that one, right kid?"*

*I laugh at him, and shake my head, explaining that A is Tate's girl.*

*"Does she know that?" Dad asks me with a grin.*

*I slap him on the back, and we continue working. Even though I usually tell my father everything, I don't share with him that I have already been daydreaming about the two of us living together in this house when it is done, raising a family in it together.*

"What are you thinking about?"

A's soft voice returns me to the present.

"The night you showed up on my front porch the first summer," I say into the top of her head, and even though I can't see her face, I know she is smiling.

She turns her head to face me, curling her body tighter to mine.

"A, I was in love with you then, I'm in love with you now and I will always be in love with you. And you may think you are different now, but I love all of you. I am in love with you when we fight and when you get angry with me. I am in love with you when you walk away from me and count the minutes until you're back in my arms. I am in love with you when you're being stubborn and I'm in love with you when you cry. The way I feel about you doesn't change if you're not perfect all the time or happy all the time. I don't expect you to be. You went through something that I wish you never had to, but no matter how much I want to change that for you, it happened. Of course, it's going to change how you feel or think about things. Your world isn't the safe one it used to be, and things don't make sense. A huge part of your life is missing and someone you love very much was taken from you. You have to talk about it, even if it's not with me, so that you can figure out a way to deal with everything you're feeling and everything you've been through. You can't keep everything inside all the time because it will eat away at you."

She nods and looks out the window.

"Sometimes, I feel like it already has. Then I have days like today and I feel like there's still part of the old me in there — the part of me that can have fun and relax like I don't have a care in the world. But there's always the guilt waiting for me. I feel guilty about so many things, Jase, but I especially feel guilty when I forget, even if it's for a little while, because I feel like I'm forgetting him, too. I feel guilty when I laugh because how can I laugh when he's not here laughing with me. I feel guilty when we're all having fun as a group, because how can we forget that he's not having fun with us. I feel guilty because how can I go on with life knowing that those three are out there enjoying theirs while Tate no longer can. I'm so angry, Jase, and I'm incredibly sad. Sometimes when we're not together and I'm sitting at the cemetery or at home in New York, I wonder how I'm ever going to be happy again. But you always remind me that it's possible. I just don't want whatever is poisoning me to poison you, too."

*Is that what she thinks? That she's poisoning me?*

I sigh out loud and A glances at me before looking out the window again. It breaks my heart to hear her say these things. I know that it's hard for her to open up to me like this. I know she doesn't like feeling that she can't take on everything by herself but knowing that she needs me and hearing her say it out loud only makes me fall more in love with her. All I want to do is kiss her and make it all better for her, but I know that I can't. I feel helpless and it makes me frustrated and angry, too.

I pull her gaze back to me and there is one lonely tear streaming down her right cheek. I brush it away with my thumb.

"It's okay to cry, babe."

She starts to shake her head, but I take her face in my hands and pull her close to mine, so our noses and foreheads touch.

"It makes me feel weak, and I'm so damn tired of feeling weak."

I shake my head against hers.

"You are the strongest person I know. I know you feel like you're in pieces right now, but I love every single one. I want to help you put them back together, but you don't need me to. You're going to find a way to do it on your own. I love you, A. I know you feel like you can't believe in much anymore, but you can believe in that. I. Love. You."

I plant small kisses on her eyelids between each word. She opens her eyes and parts her lips when my mouth travels to hers. Her eyes flutter closed again as I continue to kiss her. She pulls away from me briefly, moving her lips to my ear.

"I love you, too," she whispers softly. "Promise me that no matter what happens — you'll remember that I will never stop loving you."

I don't know that I fully understand what she's asking me to promise. I start to question her, but as she pulls away from me, I see the pleading look in her eyes and it makes me stop.

"Promise me?"

My left hand travels down her side and to her lower back holding her to me because I'm suddenly afraid that she's going to flee. My right hand brushes the side of her face as I look into her eyes.

"I promise, but I won't ever get tired of hearing you say it. Promise me the same, that you'll always remember that I love you — no matter what."

She's quiet for a moment and I'm worried that I've managed to say the wrong thing.

"Always."

She says it so quietly that I almost miss it. My hand pulls her face in closer again. She kisses me lightly before returning her head to my chest. She doesn't say another word, but as we both drift off to sleep, I can feel warm tears pool on my shirt underneath her.

# 11 – Ayla

I peek my head into the open doorway of Jase's office. He's sitting in front of his computer reading something. I can tell because he moves his mouth as if he's reading out loud, a habit I've always thought to be adorable.

I stand still for a moment watching him. One of his recent projects, a custom jewelry cabinet, lays unfinished on its side on top of his workbench. There are drawings of it at every angle pinned to the board above it. On the other side of the room are framed photos of various projects that he's completed over the past few years.

I can't see what he is reading from where I'm standing, but I do see that it is something about Sam Maloof, the famous woodworker and furniture designer. I'm not surprised, as Sam is one of Jase's heroes. Above the computer hangs a signed photo of him. His father gave him the photo for his birthday last year and I think it's one of Jase's most prized possessions. Jase has studied Sam's work since he was young and has read his biography so many times that the pages no longer lay flat on their own. It was the biography that had given him the idea to reuse the salvaged pieces of wood from the renovation house to make chairs for the dining room and front porch.

I walk up behind him and put both hands on his shoulders, massaging in large, slow circles. He leans back into me but continues to read whatever is on the screen.

"Breakfast is ready," I whisper into his ear.

I kiss the top of his head and walk back to the kitchen, where two omelets are sitting on plates, steam rising from them. I pour orange juice into two empty mugs as Jase walks into the kitchen, a goofy smile on his face and excitement lit in his eyes.

"Sam Maloof Woodworker offered me a training fellowship next year!"

He scoops me up in his arms and spins me around in a circle. His excitement is contagious.

"Jase, that's wonderful! That is a dream come true for you! I didn't know you applied. Why didn't you tell me?"

I look into his eyes and see a flicker of emotion.

"I didn't tell anyone I was applying except for dad. It seems kind of silly in the grand scheme of things. With everything else that's going on … "

Jase pauses and my heart drops. Sometimes even I can't get over how self-absorbed I can be. I reach out to him and Jase grabs my hand but waves off my apology before I can offer it.

"I wasn't sure I even had a shot. I had to pass a long admissions process and they only accept five people, but I'm one of the five. I can't believe I am going to be trained on the grounds that Sam lived on. I've been dreaming about this since I was ten!"

I nod and squeeze him to me as I think about the hours he would spend studying the rocking chairs that Maloof is famous for.

"As if you didn't have a shot. Please," I say to him, shoving him playfully. "I'm so proud of you!"

Jase dances around the kitchen with me in his arms. I can't help but laugh out loud.

"I have to fill out paperwork and send a final portfolio of five of my best projects. There's a phone interview and an online orientation sometime in the spring. The fellowship takes place for a few months in California next summer."

I instantly feel my stomach drop. I bite back the selfish words that make me want to scream that summer is our time together. I shove down the worry that sets in with the realization of spending an entire summer apart. We stop dancing and sit down in front of our eggs and juice.

"Would you help me choose which projects to send in the portfolio? I'm going to ask dad, too."

Jase's smile widens as he reaches for my hand. His right knee bounces up and down with excitement.

"Of course," I say.

I place a forkful of cheese and eggs into my mouth so that I don't have to say anything else. We eat our breakfast as Jase tells me about the fellowship in detail. By the time breakfast is over and I finish washing the dishes, Jase is already on the phone with his father talking about it. I grin to myself at the kitchen sink as I listen to Jase's voice rise with excitement and swallow the lump in my throat. I try not to think about spending a summer in Virginia without Tate and now without

Jase, too. I think about last night and our conversation and how I cried myself to sleep in his arms.

I finish drying the pan I used to make the omelets and head toward Jase's office trying to feel as excited about this as Jase is. He's spent years working hard while the rest of us goofed off. He's followed Sam Maloof's work, tirelessly studying his techniques. He's been renovating a house since the age when most kids are simply learning to drive.

*So why can't I be excited for him instead of panicked about what it means for me?*

This is a once in a lifetime opportunity, and Jase, of all people, deserves it.

# 12 - Jase

Ayla and I spend the entire morning condensing projects for my portfolio. I still can't believe that this is really happening. I applied months ago, but I didn't want to get my hopes up.

*I am going to be a fellow with Sam Maloof Woodworker, Inc.*

I keep repeating it to myself. I've had the same goofy grin plastered on my face all morning. I look over at A and can't help but think that this is the start of good things for us. I watch her as we sift through photos, and when she catches me, I lean over and kiss her.

I called dad earlier and he told me to bring the portfolio with me to dinner tonight. I ask Ayla to join us, but she insists that she doesn't want to impose. I shake my head when she says things like that, because I think my father is as comfortable around her as I am, but I don't argue. Not today. I don't want to start a fight. Today is a good day. I felt it when I woke up, even before I found out about the fellowship.

And as I drop A off at the summerhouse, I feel like everything is falling into place and working out the way that it's supposed to. That is, until I glance in the rearview mirror and watch Jesse greet her with a lingering hug, an open bottle of liquor in one hand. I keep my eyes trained in the rearview, watching A slip out of the hug and grab for the bottle of whiskey. She takes a long swig before hopping onto Jesse's back and I watch as he carries her behind the house.

Jealousy climbs over me, clumsy and heavy. I try to convince myself that I'm being ridiculous, but as I pull out of the driveway and onto the road, there's a heavy feeling rooted in my stomach now.

I try not to think about A and what she is doing or how much she is drinking as I sit down for dinner with dad. I tell him more about the fellowship program, but he can tell right away that I'm preoccupied with other thoughts. He asks me about it, but I brush him off.

"I'm going to say this only once, son, because I think it warrants being said. You know that I think the world of Ayla, and I know that you love her, but this is a once in a lifetime opportunity. Don't let anything going on with her keep you from enjoying every moment of this. You worked damn hard to get here. You should be flying high tonight and celebrating, but instead you're sitting here with your old man, brow furrowed like you're carrying the weight of the world on your shoulders. Don't let anyone take this away from you."

He raises a glass to me and nods before taking a small sip of the amber liquid. As his words sink in, I realize that dad always knows what's on my mind without me having to say it out loud. I'm reminded that he's been through similar things with mom. He knows that I worry about Ayla the same way. As I take a sip of my own drink, I remember the first time I realized how worried for mom he actually was.

*The bus drops me off at the end of my long driveway and kicks up a cloud of dry dust as it pulls away. I sling my backpack a bit higher on my shoulder as I look around before continuing to the house. Pop usually meets me at the end of the driveway so we can chat about the school day on the walk back to the house. The fact that I'm walking alone with my father nowhere in sight worries me, my stomach churning in knots, knowing that means one thing — mom is missing again.*

*This has been happening more and more lately, and while I don't understand where she goes, she almost always comes home stinking like the burn of cigarettes and alcohol. I worry about her, but not the same way Pop does. I worry more about him, because mom's drinking seems to take more of a toll on him than her. She always crawls out of bed the next morning like she never left us at all, but I can see it slowly taking pieces of him each time it happens.*

*I don't understand her, but I don't know if I ever really have. Even before I remember the drinking or the disappearing, I've always known my mother to be a complicated person. She's beautiful and loves the attention she gets from other people because of it. She likes things her way, and doesn't like to compromise, but always likes to remind me that she'll compromise for Pop. She loves to play with me outside, hates doing any kind of housework, and has always said that sunshine heals us from the woes of the world. She also has a short fuse, is sad most of the time without me fully understanding why and is frustrated by conversation often. I've learned to stay quiet when she is mad and try my hardest to keep her smiling. So does Pop, but it never seems to last long.*

*Now I don't talk to mom much. I tell dad everything instead, but I don't talk to him about mom or that I'm scared when she's gone that she's not going to come home. When I started middle school, I learned that talking to dad about mom's drinking was the one topic he wasn't ready to hear about from me. He snapped at me, something he almost never does, and I haven't brought it up since. Even on days like today, when she's nowhere to be found and he's obviously worried about it.*

*I open and close the front door of the house and can hear dad talking on the phone in the back room. I walk up to the closed door without opening it, resting my ear against the wood. I can hear him talking about mom — that he doesn't know what to do for her anymore. I hear the sadness in his voice and feel the desperation through the thick wood. It tugs at my heart and the second I hear him hang up the phone, I knock softly on the door.*

*The door swings open and my Pops — a man who I've never seen cry in my life — is standing before me with tears in his eyes. It's enough to stop every word caught in my throat. I stand there, silent and unmoving for a moment, unsure of what to say or do. I look down at my feet, not wanting to embarrass him, and then I do the only thing I can think of — I step forward and hug him. My head is almost to his chest now, but his strong arms wrap me up in a tight hug like he used to when I was little. They keep me there for at least ten minutes, and I stay strong and still within his embrace even though I want to break and cry. When he finally takes a step back, the tears are gone and I'm thankful for it. He quickly kisses the top of my head — something else he hasn't done since I was very small — and tells me he's heading to the garage for a bit.*

I finish the rest of dinner, more lost in thought than before, but now dad's thoughts are lost with ghosts of the past as well.

After dinner, he walks me to my truck and pulls me into an unexpected tight hug before I open the driver side door. His arms hold me close, and I feel choked up for a moment as the memory from earlier hits me harder this time. He pulls back as abruptly as he pulled me in, and his eyes are sad, but he's smiling.

As I pull out of the driveway, I yell out the window.

"Love you, Pop."

He nods as he usually does, his way of returning the sentiment. I leave him standing in the driveway, but his words and my memories stay with me long after I leave.

# 13 - Ayla

I watch Jase back out of the driveway. I wave to him as Jesse walks out the front door of the summerhouse and grasps me in a tight hug. I laugh into his shoulder and can feel the burn of whiskey on his breath.

"Where's lover boy going?" Jesse says to me with a grin and a hint of sarcasm, pointing a thumb over his shoulder at Jase's truck.

"He's having dinner with his dad tonight," I say and take the open bottle from his hand when he offers it to me.

I lean my head back and let the whiskey fill my mouth as the fumes burn every part of my throat. I swallow it, forgetting about Jase and the fellowship as Jesse tells me to hop on his back. He carries me, piggyback style, into the backyard as I drink more. This time, I cough as it burns its way to my stomach, but there is something about the pain that I enjoy.

Everyone is scattered across the backyard. Ace is building a fire pit in the sand while Ryan flips something on the grill. The smell of charcoal fills the air around me, and I can hear laughter as Alex, Jackson and Zac throw a football in the grass. Mikey and Austin are carrying armfuls of wood toward Ace. Ashleigh is setting the picnic table with paper plates and utensils.

I wrap my arms tighter around Jesse's neck and hand the bottle back to him. He walks to the deck and lets me hop off his back. He immediately chugs more whiskey as he slings an arm over my shoulder.

"Rocky!" I hear Alex call from where he stands, and I shake my head at him.

*He never gets tired of that nickname.*

Ryan waves one of the biggest metal spatulas I've ever seen and asks, "Dog, burger, or both?"

I shrug.

"Surprise me!" I tell him, thinking to myself that I'm not that hungry.

I reach for the whiskey again, but before Jesse can hand it over, Ashleigh hands me a drink in a red plastic cup.

"Try this instead of the gasoline that Jesse is drinking."

I smile gratefully at Ashleigh as she saunters back to where Ryan is standing in front of the grill. I face Jesse with raised eyebrows as he scrunches his face and mimics her speaking. I slap him playfully and try to stifle a laugh as I take a sip of the yellow liquid that fills the cup. It's sweet and tastes like lemons. I can tell there is vodka in it by the burn on my tongue, but it's nothing compared to the whiskey.

"This is pretty good," I tell Jesse and hand him the cup.

He takes one sip, spits it out on the ground and shakes his head.

"Too sweet. That shit will make you sick, A," he says, and walks away toward the beach with the whiskey in hand. I watch him as he helps Ace, never letting go of the bottle.

I walk up the steps and sit at the table with Ashleigh, thanking her for the drink. By the time the hot dogs and hamburgers are ready, Ashleigh and I have finished a couple of lemonades. My mind is now far away from Jase and his fellowship. Everything feels soft and smooth. I find myself smiling as Ashleigh giggles at everything Ryan says.

Everyone sits at the picnic table. Ace takes the bottle of whiskey from Jesse, who's finished almost half of it on his own. He pours some into his cup of soda and hands it to Zac who does the same. I fill two more cups of Ashleigh's lemonade mix for the both of us as the whiskey bottle makes its way around the table.

"To Tate," Zac says, nodding his head at Ryan, but holding his drink up in the air for all of us to join.

"To Tate!" we say in unison and continue to drink.

I feel tears in the back of my throat at the mention of Tate's name, but swallow them with my lemonade. When everyone else puts their cup on the table, I lean my head farther back and finish what's left in mine. I watch as Jesse does the same with the open bottle. He didn't bother to fill a cup. I hear Ace whisper angrily to Jesse, probably telling him to slow down. Jesse rolls his eyes, hands the bottle over to Ace and takes a bite of the hamburger that's in front of him.

I look at the cheeseburger that Ryan places in front of me as my stomach dips. I push it away from me and get up to make more lemonade. Inside the kitchen, I can see the picnic table from the window above the sink. I watch the boys as they eat, and Jesse looks up to smile at me through the window. I blow him a kiss as I pour lemonade mix, water and what would probably be considered too much vodka into the large glass container next to the sink. I stir the mixture a few times before I make a second pitcher of regular lemonade without vodka and stir that. Zac walks into the house with two empty hot dog rolls in hand as I'm finishing mixing the second pitcher. He hands me both rolls and I look back at him with raised eyebrows.

"I noticed you didn't eat your burger. Eat these. You'll thank me later."

I break off a piece of the roll to eat it without arguing. Zac laughs at me as I fill both cheeks with bread and smile. I catch my reflection in the window and laugh, too.

"So, what's this concoction you're making taste like?" he says to me and hands me an empty cup.

I fill it to the very top for him.

"It's spiked lemonade and Ashleigh made it the first time around. It's pretty good."

I watch as Zac swallows loudly and immediately scrunches his face.

"A — that tastes like lemon-flavored vodka!"

He shakes his head at me, but this doesn't stop him from taking another sip. I fill my cup and then fill another from the non-alcoholic pitcher.

"What's in that one?" Zac asks, eyeing me curiously.

"It's for Ashleigh. It's regular lemonade, but I'm not sure she'll know the difference. I think she's pretty drunk already and probably could use some hydration," I say to Zac with a large grin.

We walk out the sliding door together, Zac's laughter echoing around us.

"What are you two so happy about?" Ryan asks, peering over his beer.

"Zac was admiring Ashleigh's lemonade. You made something special, Ash!" I say as I hand her cup to her and hear Zac laugh again.

"A, I don't think Ashleigh needs anymore," I hear Ryan say behind me.

I watch Ashleigh make a face at him as she grabs for the cup and takes a long sip.

*Maybe I'm not the only one who hates being told what to do.*

Zac leans down and whispers in Ryan's ear. Ryan puts his arm around Ashleigh as she takes another sip, but winks at me when she isn't looking. I wink back and we walk to where some of the others are gathered around the fire.

The fire is surrounded by lawn chairs or overturned wooden crates that were found on the beach. Zac hops into one of the open chairs and pats the one next to him for me to sit in. I sit down and Ryan lowers himself on top of the cooler on the other side of me. Ashleigh quickly hops onto his lap.

Jesse has his guitar, and despite the large amounts of whiskey he has consumed, proceeds to play like he hasn't had a drink at all. He finishes one song and starts another. When he plays a song that we all know, we chime in and sing with him, but mostly we let Jesse sing alone.

*Tonight is a good night even though Jase isn't here.*

Maybe a summer without Jase won't be as bad as I think it will be, but the tug at my heart says otherwise. I stare into the fire fighting the sudden threat of tears that has risen in my throat.

I swallow hard, trying to swallow the tears, and look up as Jesse starts another song. I look over at Alex as he joins in, very obviously out of tune, and laugh with some of the others. Alex gives us the finger, but continues to sing, loudly. I look down at my lap and grin, wishing the inside of me matched the expression on my face.

*How is it possible to feel so alone when I'm surrounded by all of my friends?*

# 14 - Jase

I pull up to the summerhouse shortly after the sun goes down. I can hear the echo of laughter through the open windows in my truck and head to the back of the house.

The fire comes into view and my stomach twists when I don't see A's face among the group. I know sitting around the fire is usually paired with hours of drinking, and when A drinks she usually ends up at the cemetery.

I hate that she loves to walk everywhere, completely oblivious to how dangerous it can be at night. We fight a lot about that, but most of those fights end with her walking anyway and me being furious about it.

We haven't always seen eye to eye on everything. In the past, we've always had conversations where we challenged each other with different perspectives, but now our arguments typically push us farther apart. Now I worry about her constantly, which she finds annoying.

I approach the fire quietly and startle Ashleigh when I say hello to everyone. She is on Ryan's lap, but jumps in the air at the sound of my voice and ends up in the sand. This makes everyone laugh, me included, and I forget the nervousness in my stomach for a moment. Ryan helps Ashleigh up as she dusts the sand off her legs, and I mumble a quick apology. She bats her eyelashes at me and smiles, placing a hand on my arm to tell me it's okay. I help myself to a beer in the now open cooler, since Ryan is no longer sitting on it.

I try not to immediately ask about A, but as usual, Ryan can read my expression.

"She took off to head to the cemetery, but Jesse is with her so she's not alone."

I nod and look into my beer, the jealousy from before seeping into my limbs. I clench my jaw and force myself to stay still in front of the fire instead of running back to my truck to find her like my instincts are screaming at me to do. This is an internal battle I have constantly now.

Alex continues telling the story that I interrupted when I walked up. In a few moments, everyone else is caught up in the story as I sit down in an empty lawn chair next to Zac. Alex is telling his story, his arms moving animatedly. I missed the first half but laugh with everyone else when Alex gets to the punch line.

I open another beer, all the while keeping my eyes trained on the back door and the side of the house waiting for Ayla and Jesse to return. They are still gone when I reach into the cooler for a third beer.

Alex and Ace walk to the house to fill the cooler again as Zac tells me about the latest girl he's hooked up with. He tells these crazy hook-up stories that make Ashleigh roll her eyes at him disapprovingly. Sometimes I think he may embellish them just to get a rise from her, but then again, you never know with Zac.

When Alex and Ace carry the cooler back to the fire, Ryan doles out fresh beers to everyone. I have been drinking mine faster than I normally do, but I'm celebrating tonight. I excitedly tell the guys about the fellowship and Zac slaps me on the back with a grin.

"That's great, Jase. You'll have to remember us when you're famous!"

There is laughter all around. I shake my head at Zac but can't hide the grin from my face. The only one who hasn't said anything is Ryan. He looks worried, but I have no idea why.

Ryan pulls me aside, away from the rest of the group.

"How does A feel about the fellowship?" Ryan asks me.

I give him a funny look, turning my head to the side.

"What do you mean? She's excited, of course."

I take another drink, feeling the cold all the way to my stomach.

"Jase, you'd be spending an entire summer in California. The summer is the only time you guys get to see each other every day."

Ryan looks at me as though that should have been obvious.

"Well, I just assumed she'd come with me, Ry."

"But that means you'd both be gone all summer."

I smile at Ryan, not understanding his point and thinking maybe he had a few too many drinks tonight.

"Yup, it does."

Ryan's eyes lock with mine and the usual playfulness is gone, replaced with intense concern.

"But summer is all of ours … we always spend them together. Not just you and A — all of us."

I feel like shit because that thought hadn't even occurred to me. Guilt spreads through me, coursing through my limbs with an intense heat, or maybe that is just the alcohol kicking in.

"I hadn't thought about it like that," I say softly, the excitement in the air now dead.

We're standing about twenty feet from the fire and an awkward silence hangs in the air. I don't know what to say and I'm not sure he does either.

"Hey, handsome."

The voice behind me makes me smile before I turn around. Ayla wraps her arms around me and I turn in her embrace. She kisses me briefly and she tastes sweet, like cherry Chapstick and lemons.

I don't bring up the cemetery or the fact that I've been anxiously waiting for her to return. I smile down at her, simply grateful she's back in my arms.

"We hear a celebration is in order," Ryan's voice interrupts my thoughts.

I realize the concern is gone now, his eyes back to smiling. Ayla smiles right back at him, beaming.

"It sure is! I'm so proud of him," she says and looks straight into my eyes with such an intense stare that I swear she can see right into the deepest parts of me.

Ryan nods his head.

"We all are," he says, slinging his arm around my shoulder.

But Ryan has planted the seed and now I can feel the roots of doubt digging into my brain. My head is swimming with too much beer and guilt, unsure how Ayla really feels about the fellowship. I wonder if she thought about coming with me or staying back to spend the summer with everyone else. Maybe she hasn't thought that far ahead yet. But I had assumed she would come with me. I consider the idea of attending the fellowship without her, but the vision doesn't feel the same — it loses the excitement it offers without her to share it with me.

The fire continues to burn as the moon rises higher in the sky. Dad's words are still lingering in my head. There are conversations all around me, but I haven't been a participant in any of them. I sit next to Ayla, holding her hand, but lost in thought for the rest of the night, unsure of how I feel about the fellowship at all anymore.

# 15 - Ayla

When everyone else goes inside to sleep, I watch Jase as he stares at the sky lost in thought. My hand hasn't left his, but he seems far away from me tonight. Now that it's just the two of us, I ask him softly what's on his mind.

He looks at me briefly and smiles, and then stares out over the water in front of us.

"How do you really feel about the fellowship?"

I'm surprised by the question and immediately feel my face blush, betraying me.

"I'm excited for you, of course! Why?"

My hand is still tangled with his, but I pull it away, trying to get him to look at me. It works and he does, feeling the loss of connection as quickly as I do. He looks down at our hands and then into my eyes.

"Had it crossed your mind that we would be spending the summer apart?" he asks, his voice tipping into frustration.

I silently wonder how to respond to this. I know either answer is not going to give him what he wants in the moment — what he probably needs.

"Yes, of course I have. But this is such an awesome opportunity that us being apart shouldn't matter."

Jase shakes his head slowly and sadly. I feel like I've failed whatever test he was offering.

"Ayla, I assumed you would come with me."

I'm surprised and he can see it in my face.

"Did you really think I'd leave for three months and not want you with me?"

I consider this for a moment. The thought honestly hadn't occurred to me. I assumed he hadn't thought about it at all, lost in the excitement of being accepted.

But there are so many reasons I can't go with him, and I know that none of them are going to be ones that he'll understand.

"Jase—" I say, and he can hear my answer in my tone before I say another word.

"You don't want to come with me?" he cries, sounding wounded in a way that slices right through my heart.

I place both hands on either side of his face. I make him look into my eyes, unblinking.

"You need to do this for you, Jase. I can't go with you. But you need to do this."

He pulls his face out of my grasp before I can say any more.

"You can't or you won't?" he asks me, pleading for me to offer him more.

"Jase, I'll still be in school when you have to leave, and I have to be here for the summer for the Gematti's. I can't go to California, but I can come visit. We all can."

I look at him, hopeful that is enough for him, but his expression says otherwise.

"You have to be here for the Gematti's?" he asks me.

I look down at my hands and try think of a better way to explain it. He grabs for my hand and forces me to look him in the eye. I know what he wants me to say out loud. I know when I do, it will make him angry.

"I can't leave Tate, Jase. I don't want to be away from him for the entire summer."

Jase's face twists and I know I've hurt him. He snorts and shakes his head.

"Well, that's great, A, because I don't want to be away from you for the entire summer. But apparently that doesn't matter as much to you."

My heart sinks. That's not how I meant it to come out, but I know there is some truth in it. I don't want to be without Jase for the summer. It was my first thought when he told me about the fellowship. But if the choice comes down to go with him to California or stay here to be with Tate and everyone else, I have to choose here. It's not a choice for me. It just is.

"I don't want this to change how you feel about the fellowship, my love. I want you to be as excited about it as you were this morning when you told me. This isn't about me and you. This is about you and your future."

Jase is visibly angry now, his hands in fists at his side.

"You are my future, A. I'm just not sure if I'm yours anymore."

"How can you say that?"

"Because you're choosing to stay behind with everyone else instead of coming with me. What else does that mean?"

"Jase, I can't leave Tate—"

"A, Tate is dead!"

Jase's voice echoes into the sky. It fills my ears and my mind goes blank. I don't feel anything — no anger or sadness, just nothing. I'm empty. I'm a dark and endless cavern that used to be filled with so many things, but now is only hollow.

I look at him and say nothing, because there is nothing left to say.

He falls to his knees in the sand in front of me and I crawl forward until our bodies are touching. He's breathing heavy as I pull him close to me, wrapping my arms tight around him and trying to hold him together when I know that all I'm really doing is tearing him apart.

# 16 - Jase

I toss and turn all night, not able to fully drift off to sleep. The sun is just starting to rise when I quietly climb out of bed, careful not to wake Ayla. I look down at her and the pain in my chest magnifies. My head is a mess, and I spent all night spinning over questions that Ayla can't seem to answer for me, so I quickly get dressed and head to my truck instead.

I drive to the renovation house and head straight into the office to work on design plans. I try to keep my hands and mind busy so that my thoughts aren't consumed by Ayla and what our conversation from last night means for our relationship.

I don't want to be selfish. I don't expect her to simply follow me everywhere I go, but this is a once in a lifetime opportunity for me — something I've dreamed about since I was a kid — and I want her to be part of it. She hadn't even considered coming with me. She told me it isn't an option for her and that she wants me to go, but what she couldn't answer is what that means for us. I know she's been pulling away from me, but she's been pulling away from all of us. I never considered her heart may not be in the same place as mine.

I wanted to ask her a million questions last night while we kneeled in the sand, her arms wrapped around me. I wanted to demand answers, but she didn't seem to have any to offer me. For the first time, I didn't feel like she was holding back or trying to hide anything she was feeling. She seemed like she wasn't feeling anything at all, and that may have been worse for me. How can she have nothing to say — nothing to feel — when it comes to us being apart? I don't understand even though I desperately want to, but we went to bed with no answers and no explanation.

I held her all night while my mind raced, but I couldn't sleep. I have this sinking feeling in my chest that all of her non-answers are really answers I am not ready to hear.

I've always had to compete with Tate in some way, even when he was alive. The beginning of our relationship started as a secret because everyone thought that Ayla and Tate were together — something they went along with to help Tate hide the fact that he was gay from his father and brother, and well, all of us. That was not easy to deal with at times, but this?

*I don't know what to do with this.*

Ayla is still choosing Tate even though he's gone — dead — and I don't know what that means for us or for me.

I don't know what is fair to ask of her and I don't want to ask too much, but the casual way she brushes off us not being together and not seeing each other next summer hurts me in a way that she doesn't realize.

It makes a part of me not want to do the fellowship at all, but the idea and willingness to give up on that dream crushes me in a different way. I don't want to regret it or resent her for it, and I know that eventually I would.

*Apparently, I don't have any answers either.*

I take a deep breath and try to focus on the drawing in front of me. I get to work at the bench, momentarily quieting all of the thoughts about Ayla and the fellowship in California and let the slab of wood and visions of what it could be fill my head instead.

Everyone has always commented on what a hard worker I am — how I never seem to know how to relax or rest because my mind is always on the next project I need to take on. What no one realizes is that building, designing, putting things together and being able to see what things can be instead of what they are has been a way for me to work through things in my life. Some people go to therapy. Dad and I have always worked — constructed beautiful things out of materials other people would throw away or toss aside.

*It's late, but I can't sleep. My mind is racing, and I can hear the echo of my parents' voices rising from downstairs along with the occasional sound of broken glass. Despite the fact that he's had to replace our glasses and a few dishes on multiple occasions, Pop doesn't stop mom from throwing them at him when she's angry. She missed dinner again tonight, and when she came home staggering up the porch steps, Pop wouldn't meet my eyes. I excused myself and walked to my bedroom as he opened the front door to help her inside. They've been fighting ever since, although it's mostly mom's voice that I hear. I don't know why mom is so unhappy or why she doesn't want to spend time with us anymore, but there are days where I pray that she makes it back to us safely and other days I wish she would just leave us for good for Pops' sake. Honestly, in many ways, she's already left us, but I always feel guilty for wishing that.*

*I hear another large shattering sound and then a door slam. It sounds like Pop went out to the garage, his way of escaping lately. I walk down the stairs slowly and can hear mom crying before I hit the bottom step. Her head is in her arms and she is leaning over the side of the couch sobbing. I grab a blanket from the chair next to her and wrap it lightly around her shoulders, but she jolts upright as I do.*

*"Can't you see that I want to be left alone?!"*

*The anger in her voice makes me jump backward. For a moment, she looks guilty for the outburst, but she returns her head to her arms and continues to sob, louder this time. I don't know how to help her, and I don't think she wants me to.*

*Even though it's way past my bedtime and I have school in the morning, I sneak outside instead of going back up to my room. I see the light on inside the garage and open the door silently. Pop is hunched over his workbench, using the circular saw. I know enough not to startle him while it's on, so I wait until he stops and takes a step back before I clear my throat behind him. He doesn't jump at the sound, just waves at me over his shoulder to come closer like he knew I was there all along.*

*He doesn't say anything about mom or their fight. He talks about the wood in front of him and what he is building. He explains to me how important it is to see what things can be and that woodworking is about being able to see the beauty in all of the fine lines, the grain, and even the cracks because it's what makes each piece unique.*

*We stand side by side for another hour, just the two of us in the garage separate from the outside world, our hands keeping busy so that our minds can be silent.*

Dad and I build when others want to give up and walk away. And that's why the renovation house has been such a passion project of mine. Dad and I found a beautiful piece of property with an old farmhouse that hadn't been taken care of in years and I knew right away I would buy it. As dad said, it has good bones. The foundation is strong, but everything else was a bit of a mess.

*Kind of like the way Ayla and I are right now.*

I like throwing myself into something that I can make better. I like going to sleep at night knowing that I helped make something beautiful again. I don't understand not wanting to make something better rather than feed into making it worse. I don't understand destroying things or giving up on them or yourself.

I'm not ready to give up on Ayla and our relationship. I don't think I ever will be. But I'm worried that she is starting to, or maybe she already has. Her first instinct has always been to walk away any time things are difficult for her, which has always been tough for me because my first instinct is to figure out how I can fix it or make it better. I'm terrified because I'm learning there are some things I can't fix. There are some things I can't make better for her or for us, and maybe that's something she's known for a while now.

# 17 – Ayla

I wake up slowly, stretching my arms and legs before fully opening my eyes. I know immediately that the other side of the bed is empty. The second that I'm fully awake, my body can recognize the loss of Jase's presence. I reach over to his side of the bed and it's cool to the touch which means he must have left a while ago. I'm surprised I didn't wake up, as I usually startle easily while asleep.

There's a part of me that fights with myself every single morning to get out of bed. I usually wake up, glance at the time and ask myself why I should even get up at all. I question what the point is of getting out of bed today. If it weren't for what my friends and my family would think, I probably would stay in bed all day. I usually don't feel like dealing with their judgements or their comments, so I use every bit of energy I have to force myself out of bed and into the shower.

Some days are worse than others. On the easier days, I get in the shower angrily resenting the fact that I have to keep up appearances rather than sink into the sadness that seeps its way into every edge of my life now. Those are the easy days, because anger is always easier for me. On the especially difficult days, I stand in the shower underneath the hot water and go completely blank. My mind doesn't wander. I don't have an internal conversation with myself. I disappear into nothing. I stand and stare at the small chip in the shower wall until the water turns cold. I lose track of time. Sometimes Jase, or mom if I'm home, will knock on the door to snap me back to reality and I have no sense of how much time has passed.

It scares me that I can completely zonk out like that. I'm not sure where I go. Maybe it's an escape for my brain when it doesn't want to deal with anything anymore.

I find myself doing this more and more outside of the shower, too. If I'm alone, I stare off into space and lose myself in it.

If I'm being completely honest, I want to be alone more and more. Being around people, even my closest friends, makes me feel like I have to constantly put on a show. I'd rather not have to explain myself or rationalize what I'm feeling. I'd rather not have to pretend. I'd rather be alone and live in the silence. It's easier to be alone. When I'm in a setting where there are a lot of people, I daydream about heading home and crawling back into bed, pulling the covers over my head and sleeping the day or night away. There are times that I do just that.

On the worst days, something small triggers me immediately back to the road with Tate that night and I can't stop it. A sound or a smell hits me out of nowhere and before long I'm trembling from head to toe and tears are streaming down my face. I can't fully explain why to anyone around me. No one else understands. No one else gets it. So, it's easier to be alone where I don't have to hide my trembling hands or run to the bathroom to pull myself out of a panic attack. It's easier to be alone when I feel like I can't breathe and everything is closing in around me.

*I'm a damn mess.*

I shake my head at my reflection in the mirror, swiping at the steam from the shower so my face looks distorted in the reflection. That's a more accurate depiction of how I feel.

*Distorted.*

I want it to all go away. I want to go back to the days when my biggest stressors were school and grades and boys. I want to go back to before Tate died, when my life was pretty close to perfect and I didn't realize it or appreciate it.

I'm exhausted all of the time. My body and mind need a break, but I don't know how to give it to them. I feel like there is constantly someone needing something from me, even if it's myself, and most days I can't or won't deal with it.

I was never a big drinker before. I had a drink or two with friends and that was all I needed or wanted. I never understood drinking to the point of getting sloppy or falling over. I secretly always thought it was what sad, pathetic people do, and now I'm one of those sad, pathetic people. I wonder how many people think that about me now. Sometimes I don't care. Other times I care too much about what people think. Even though that is an annoying habit — to care so much about what others think of me and one I don't like to admit out loud — the truth is I think that is the one thing that has kept me from staying in the darkest places for too long. My stubborn pride has always pulled me out of whatever shadowy place I've landed in. Sometimes it also puts me in that same place, but it has always brought me back out.

I don't like being a victim. I don't feel like a victim, either. The night that everything happened with Tate, he suffered the worst of it. I was barely hurt. I walked away with some bumps and bruises and he didn't get to walk away at all. His family suffers living without him. My family suffers because they have to now deal with the very angry and confused version of me, but I'm still here to deal with. When people act like I'm the victim, or talk to me like I am, I get inexplicably angry. I think it's guilt, but this is something else I've never said out loud.

I don't understand why I got to live and Tate had to die. I struggle with this every single day. I don't understand what lottery I won that he lost, or worse, why the people who attacked us chose to hurt him in the first place. There are so many things I don't understand about that night that I continue to obsess over now. There are too many things out of my control and too many answers I don't have that make all of this impossible to live with.

*How am I supposed to live with it? How do you move on from something like this? Is it even possible?*

I hear Ryan's voice, but I can't make out what he is saying. I blink my eyes a few times and shake my head again, and his voice becomes clearer.

"A? Are you okay?"

I look down and realize I'm sitting on the edge of my bed in nothing but a towel. My hair isn't even damp from the shower anymore, so I must have been sitting here for a longer time than I realized.

Ryan's sad face tugs at my heart. I want to be better for him because I know seeing me like this is killing him. It's killing everyone. I sit up straighter in bed and pull together as natural a smile as possible.

"Yea, I'm okay, Ry. Sorry. You caught me daydreaming."

I try to laugh it off as I get up and pull some clothes from one of my drawers.

"You know that feeling when you get out of a shower," I say as I turn to him. "The one where you just want to crawl back into bed without getting dressed. I was trying to convince myself not to do that."

Ryan laughs and the sadness is gone.

"I know that feeling well. I was checking to see if you knew where Jase was, and if you guys wanted to go grab some food?"

"I think Jase is probably at the reno house. He left early this morning. I'm up for some food, though. Let me get dressed and I'll meet you downstairs."

Ryan looks like he wants to say more, and I silently pray for him to turn around and leave instead. I'm not in the mood for any heart to hearts right now, and Ryan wants to have them all the time lately. Wanting to avoid them with him makes me feel like a terrible person, but I don't know if I can handle one right now.

Thankfully, he decides not to say anything. Instead, he nods and retreats from the doorway to head downstairs. I walk over to the door and close it softly, resting my forehead on the doorframe for a moment. It's exhausting trying to pretend that you're okay when you're not. And I know it's obvious to everyone around me that I'm not. It's just easier to play this game for right now.

It was two years ago and none of this is any easier to carry. Every day it somehow feels heavier and I'm not sure how much longer I can carry the weight.

# 18 - Jase

By the time I'm wrapping up the project I've been working on all day, I realize that it's almost dark again. I spent the entire day at the renovation house, basically avoiding the texts from the guys saying they were going out to eat, mostly because I knew A was going to be with them and I still have so many things I want to say to her.

My mind raced even as I was working today, something that I can usually shut off when I'm here at the house. But today it didn't stop. I keep thinking about how many times Ayla has pulled away from me. I keep thinking about how I'm the one always chasing her and always pushing her for a bit more. I think back over the course of the last year, and how many times I've pulled her back to me when maybe she only wants me to let her go.

I keep thinking about how lost she is now, constantly swimming in sadness and anger and other things that she probably doesn't understand. I've always thought of myself as a life vest for her, something strong she can hold onto when her world is falling apart. I want to be that for her. Maybe I try too hard when it isn't what she wants or needs.

I don't know what to do or say anymore, and worse, I don't know how to feel. I love her more than anyone I've ever been with. Even though she's my first serious relationship, she's the only person who has made me feel the things that I do. I can't imagine us not being together. I can't imagine her not being in my life.

What I've realized as I work through all of my thoughts is that I don't want anything in this life if it means I have to give up Ayla, but I don't know if she still wants this. I can't seem to get a read on her lately. I feel like she's constantly hiding things, unsure if it's that she doesn't know how to explain what she's feeling or if it's that she doesn't want to hurt me. Despite everything she's been through and everything she is going through, I know Ayla would never intentionally hurt me.

But if that's the only reason we're together now — because Ayla doesn't want to hurt me — I don't know what to do with that.

*I can't begin to comprehend that.*

I finish cleaning up, quickly change into clean clothes and head to the summerhouse to talk to her. I have to pull her aside and ask the questions that I need to know the answers to, even if I'm terrified of what her answers will be.

When I get to the summerhouse, I can see the flickering of the fire around the side of the house, but when I walk to the back, Ryan is the only one there.

"Hey!"

Ry hops to his feet as soon as he sees me and gives me a handshake that turns into a hug.

"Listen, man," he starts slowly, staring at his feet before meeting my eyes. "I'm really sorry about last night. I feel like an ass. That fellowship program… that's your dream, bud, and I'm so damn happy for you and proud of you. I didn't mean to knock the wind from your sails last night. That was shitty of me to do."

I slap him lightly on the back and squeeze his shoulder as we sit down next to each other at the fire.

"It's all good, Ry. It brought up some things I hadn't thought about yet, but probably would have got to on my own eventually."

Ryan shakes his head at me.

"I should have been excited for you and that's it. It's hard for me to picture a summer without you and A here. It's selfish of me, but I want our summers to stay the same. I know they can't and won't, but it doesn't stop me from wanting them to."

Ryan grins at me and it's one of those smiles that doesn't quite meet his eyes. I feel the same way.

"I agree, man. I don't want anything to change either, but it already has. Things feel different this summer. Not better or worse, but different. Besides, maybe none of us will go anywhere, and we'll all be together again next summer like always."

Ryan is shaking his head before I finish my sentence.

"You have to go, Jase. You get chosen for a program like that and you go. End of story."

"You sound like Pops," I say to him grinning. "I don't know anymore. Ayla told me last night that she can't go with me. Or won't go with me. And I don't know if I want to go if she doesn't."

Ryan stares at me until I make eye contact with him.

"Jase, you have to go. I don't want you to, but I'm telling you that you have to. With or without Ayla, you have to go."

I nod, even though my heart is still unsure. I glance around and ask Ryan where everyone else is. He says that most of the guys are either inside or at the bungalows, and that everyone would be heading back to the fire soon. He jokes about having the night off from Ashleigh because she's having a girls' night at a bar with some friends. I'm sure Ayla was invited, but passed on the invitation because the thought of a girls' night makes her skin crawl, especially with Ashleigh's friends. I smile thinking about it and watch the window to her bedroom fill with light out of the corner of my eye. Ryan notices it, too.

"Oh yeah, and A is inside playing the piano, I think? Some of the guys filled the cooler just a few minutes ago and brought it back out here before heading to change clothes. They said she was sitting at the piano."

Ryan looks at me and shrugs. I haven't heard Ayla play the piano since Tate was alive. The two of them would play together, mostly on the nights when everyone else went out when they were too young. He taught her how to play, so it's something she doesn't do often now.

Some of the guys are returning to the fire now and my conversation with Ryan stops with their return. I look up to Ayla's window, trying to decide if I should go inside and talk to her now or wait until later. I know I can't avoid the conversation, but as I watch her silhouette walk by the window, I think of the things we talked about last night and my heart sinks. I want a good night with her — one that isn't filled with uncertainty about the future or where we stand or what we're feeling. Ryan's comments have me thinking that maybe we won't have too many of these nights left — all of us around the fire. Before long, we'll be heading in different directions as life takes us toward real jobs and marriages and families. I consider tabling the conversation until tomorrow when I notice her window goes dark again, but not before I catch a glimpse of another person in the room with her. Jealousy fills every part of me as I glance at the faces around the fire and realize immediately that the other person is Jesse.

# 19 – Ayla

*I'm probably being antisocial.*

I came inside to use the restroom and sat down at the piano before heading back outside. Before I knew it, I was playing song after song, and now it's been a good twenty minutes or so. I swing my legs around the piano bench as Alex, Ace and Jesse walk through the sliding glass door. I help them fill a cooler with drinks from the fridge as Alex and Ace each grab a side of the cooler to head back outside.

I decided not to drink tonight, something that I think surprised everyone, myself included. I know Jase will make his way back to the house eventually and I want to have a clear head when he does. I don't like the way we left things last night. Everything feels unsteady and unsure, and I hate that he left this morning without me giving him what he needed to hear last night. I want to better explain what I was trying to say last night without the fuzziness brought on by all of the lemonade I had to drink.

"I can't believe you're still drinking that crap," Jesse says to me, shaking his head.

I laugh as I look down at the bottle of water in my hand.

"Water is crap?" I ask him with a grin. "I can't believe you're still drinking that," and I nod to the bottle in his hand that is almost half empty.

"Don't you start with me, now. You're the only one that doesn't give me a hard time. Because you get it."

He takes a step closer to me and I am worried by the look in his eye that he may cry. One thing I definitely can't handle while totally sober is Jesse crying.

He swallows hard and leans against the counter next to me, our shoulders touching slightly. Trying desperately to change the subject in the hopes to avoid any kind of emotional conversation right now, I ask him if he's taken any good pictures lately with his fancy camera.

Jesse always used to have a camera in his hand, and he's captured some really beautiful moments of all of us. He has a real talent for capturing moments on film without the people in the photo even noticing. But he hasn't taken many pictures lately. In fact, I haven't seen him with his camera in a very long time.

"How are you doing with the photography course you're taking?" Jesse asks me and I'm grateful he took the lead to change the course of the conversation.

I am taking an online photography course this summer to fulfill one of the requirements for my minor at school, but one of the reasons I took it is because I knew Jesse could help me. He's been giving me some pointers and helping me with some of the assignments.

"I got an A on the last project. We had to take some landscape shots and I took some amazing photos of the sunset over the water. You have to see them."

I make a motion to follow me as I head upstairs to my bedroom with Jesse a few steps behind me. I switch on the light and walk over to my desk as I flip through piles of notebooks looking for my laptop. Jesse stands in the doorway as if he's afraid to walk into my room. I look up at him and laugh.

"I'm not going to bite, Jesse. You can come in, you know."

He shrugs from the doorway but doesn't come in any further. I can't seem to locate my laptop and pace back and forth trying to think where I left it last. I notice the camera sitting on my dresser and pick that up instead. I turn it on and flip through the photos as I hand the camera to Jesse. He takes a few steps into the room, taking the camera from me, and looks through the series of shots I took.

"A, these are really great. It's hard to get the lighting right, but you managed to capture a perfect sunset photo. That's not easy."

Jesse smiles at me and hands the camera back, which I throw softly on my bed before turning the lights off again.

We walk down the stairs with Jesse in the lead. I pick up my head and am surprised to see Jase at the bottom.

"Hey, babe. I didn't know you were here!"

I smile at him but can tell immediately that something is wrong. Jesse notices it, too, and casts a questioning look over his shoulder at me.

"Yeah, surprise. I'm here." Jase says quietly.

"Uh, I'm gonna grab another drink. You guys want anything?" Jesse says to both of us, but looks only at me.

I shake my head and let Jesse walk out of the room before I ask Jase what's wrong.

"Nothing's wrong, A."

I can tell by the flatness in his voice that he is either hurt or pissed. I roll my eyes at him.

"Yeah, okay, sure." I say in frustration.

This is not how I envisioned our night starting out. I don't know what I did to piss him off already, but I can feel my own anger rising with every word we exchange.

"What's the matter, A? You don't like it when I tell you that I'm fine when I'm obviously not?"

Jase finally picks up his head and our eyes lock. Mine cloud with instant anger, knowing that he's trying to pick a fight with me, but I don't know why. I stalk down the stairs, trying to brush past him, but he reaches out and grabs me by both arms.

"Let me go, Jase. I don't feel like fighting with you right now."

I struggle to get my arms free of his grasp, but he only holds me tighter.

"What were you and Jesse doing in your room?"

The question takes me by surprise and I immediately stop struggling.

"What?" I ask Jase, my face contorting in confusion and surprise.

"I saw you two in your room together. Why was Jesse in your bedroom? And it's a little convenient that you take him there when you think I'm not here!"

Jase's voice rises as he lets go of my arms. I laugh out loud before I can stop myself.

"Are you kidding me? You're jealous of Jesse? Jase, that's insane!"

"Don't make me feel like the crazy one, A. Dammit, I never get a straight answer from you! What am I supposed to think? You never want to talk to me, but you seem to have no problem talking to Jesse about everything and anything."

"I give up. I really do. All we do is argue anymore. You're being ridiculous right now!"

Jase laughs a sarcastic, angry laugh that stings as if he's slapped me across the face. I've never seen Jase this angry with me before or maybe this is the first time I've ever seen him jealous. Regardless of how he is feeling, I think it's completely unjustified, so I cross my arms over my chest and glare at him.

He shakes his head, runs a hand through his hair, and turns away from me to look out the window. I take the opportunity to stalk past him into the kitchen. I consider grabbing a drink to calm my nerves, but I don't want to ruin what I set out to do tonight, which is not drink. I shake my head in frustration and look back at Jase who is now staring at me again. The anger in his face is gone, but it still settles deeply in his eyes.

"So, this conversation is done? You're going to go about your night like I'm not here?" Jase says, pursing his lips together so they form a tight line.

If the anger that poisons me now didn't flood my body in this moment, I would notice that Jase's eyes are filled with a mix of sadness and desperation, not anger. If I wasn't so selfish, I would stop to give him a hug and assure him that he's the only one that I want. If I wasn't so childish, I wouldn't have ignored Jase's question and instead grab Jesse's arm the second he walks through the sliding door to ask him to go to the cemetery with me.

Jesse's gaze darts back and forth between Jase and me. Before he can answer, the front door slams with such force it knocks two pictures off of the walls. I look up to see Jase's back walking to his truck through the front windows.

"What the hell was that about? What's going on between you two lately?" Jesse asks me, pulling his arm from my grasp.

"Forget it, Jesse. It's not your problem."

I walk out the front door, slamming it behind me, too. There is a cloud of dust clinging in the air left behind from Jase's truck. I bite my lower lip and swallow the tears that want to escape. I sit down on the first step and blink them back.

I hear the front door open and close quietly, and I look at my feet as Jesse sits down next to me on the step. He doesn't say a word but puts an arm around me. He doesn't ask me any more questions. He doesn't give me a hard time because I don't want to talk. We sit in silence, my head on his shoulder, staring out into the darkness in front of us.

# 20 - Jase

I peel out of the driveway and am probably doing twice the speed limit when a cop turns his lights on behind me. Cursing, I pull the truck over to the side of the road and wait for him to approach the window. The second he sees me he recognizes me. Most of the cops in town know all of us because of what happened to Tate. I think I see a flash of pity in his eyes before he takes my license and registration back to his car.

I'm only a few miles from the summerhouse. The blue and red lights flashing behind me cast an eerie glow inside my truck. I look at my reflection in the rearview mirror and shake my head. I completely lost my cool back at the house and now I'm going to get a speeding ticket.

*Perfect.*

I stare down at my hands clenched into fists in my lap. I try not to think about how furious I am with Ayla at the moment, but my racing heart won't let me. I hate when she ignores me when we're fighting. And I know she asked Jesse to take her to the cemetery to piss me off.

*It worked.*

I wanted to throw everything in the room, smash some furniture and throw a tantrum the way that she does when she's angry. Instead, I turned around and left, something I learned from her. I grip the steering wheel in anger, trying to will it to subside.

The cop walks to the side of the car just as my knuckles are turning white and hands me the license and registration back.

"You've got a clean license, Jase. I'm going to let you go with a warning tonight, but you will drive the speed limit from here on out. I won't be so forgiving next time."

He gives me a pointed look as I thank him and avoid his eyes. When he's back in his car and pulls away, I drive into town doing at least five miles under the speed limit.

I drive through the main section of town, passing storefronts and restaurants, and finally stop at a pub for a drink instead of going home. I walk inside and a cool blast of air conditioning smacks me in the face before I take a seat at the end of the bar.

The bartender is a kid named Chris who I went to school with. He nods hello and fills a chilled mug with Sam Adams without me having to ask for it. He places it in front of me and we chat about high school. I momentarily forget about A as we relive the baseball championship we won back in senior year. Chris pours me a shot of tequila and one for himself and we finish the shot together.

"Mind if I join you?" a soft, sexy voice asks from behind me.

Chris is smiling from ear to ear as he pours another round of tequila shots, pushing the third shot in front of the girl who owns the voice. I glance in her direction and realize she's looking me up and down.

Chris laughs.

"J-man, this is Jayde. She moved here last month. Jayde, meet Jase."

She offers me her hand as I mumble a hello.

"I know who you are, you know. I'm friends with Ashleigh. A group of us were here earlier, but they headed back to Ashleigh's place a little while ago. I wasn't ready to call it a night just yet."

Jayde takes a seat at the stool immediately to my left and eyes her shot.

"Cheers," I say, offering my shot glass in the air for her and Chris.

We down the tequila at the same time and Chris quickly refills my beer when the empty shot glasses are returned to the bar.

My head is swimming and I know I should leave, but I stay against my better judgment. I look at the frothy beer sitting in front of me and let it sit there for a few moments, trying to decide whether or not I want to strike up any more conversation with Jayde. Chris is at the opposite end of the bar helping other customers. Jayde starts the conversation before I can.

"I know that Ashleigh's boyfriend Ryan is your best friend. And Ashleigh is my best friend. Wait until she hears that we were drinking together tonight. Small world, right?"

Jayde smiles at me and I notice a small dimple in her chin. Her eyes are a deep shade of green and I find myself staring into them for longer than I mean to. She places her hand on my arm lightly, but her touch sends a surge of guilt through me. I immediately pull back and grab for my beer. I drink what's left of the beer as Jayde calls for Chris to pour more shots.

*I should leave. Get up right now, Jase, and go home.*

I tell my legs to move, but they don't. Chris puts three more shots of tequila on the bar and pushes one toward me. I raise the shot as Jayde and Chris do the same before I pour it into my mouth.

Jayde smiles and looks at me through long, dark eyelashes. She licks her lips softly and places her hand right next to my arm on the bar. I stare at her hand, silently willing it not to move any closer.

"You build things, right?"

Jayde's voice breaks my gaze from her hand. I feel numb.

"What?" I ask her, looking into her green eyes again.

"Isn't that what you do? You make furniture or something?" Jayde says as she giggles while Chris pours another round of tequila. "Men who work with their hands are so sexy."

She moves her hand to my arm and runs her fingers lightly over my skin as I finish my shot. This time I don't pull away as she inches closer to me on her bar stool.

# 21 - Ayla

I roll over in bed and look at the clock. I haven't fallen asleep yet, but it's already seven in the morning. The sun is shining brightly through my bedroom window. I groan, throw back the covers and sit up in bed. I check my phone. No new messages. No missed calls. My heart clenches as I sigh and drop the phone back on the dresser.

Jase and I seem to fight all the time now, but we never go to bed angry. That's his rule. We usually apologize, or just move on without talking about it and by morning everything is okay again. But he didn't call last night. He didn't show up at the house or crawl into bed next to me like he usually does. I can't remember the last time I spent the entire night without him during the summer. I bite my lip as I think about our fight last night. I replayed the argument continuously all night. I stare at the ceiling and play it over and over in my head. Sure, Jase acted out of jealousy, but I was no better. I acted like a child — again.

*I really need to grow up.*

I throw on a t-shirt and shorts, grab my sneakers and head out to the back deck. The sun is already hot, and the heat hangs heavy in the air even though it's still early in the morning. I tie my sneakers and put my headphones in as I start the four-mile run to the renovation house. My stomach is in knots as I hit the pavement of the main road. I hate apologizing, even to Jase. It makes me feel vulnerable and being vulnerable makes me feel weak.

I spend the next two miles practicing what I am going to say to Jase when I get to the house, but as I run through Main Street in town, I notice Jase's truck parked outside a bar. I stop in my tracks and stare at the truck until my vision blurs and it starts to lose its shape. I blink a few times, half expecting the truck to disappear, but it doesn't.

I sit down on a bench across the street from the bar and the truck. I pause my music and call Jase's phone. It rings four times and then his voicemail picks up.

I decide not to leave a message. It's still early, and if he was drinking until late last night, he's probably sound asleep. I jog across the street and try the driver's side door. It opens easily and I quickly find the keys hidden behind the visor. I start the truck and drive the last few miles to the renovation house. I try to open the front door of the house, but it's locked. I know where Jase hides the key, but I feel weird letting myself into the house when he's not here. I have a quick vision of him shaking his head at me, telling me that I'm acting ridiculous, but it doesn't change my mind. I leave his truck keys behind the visor where I found them and try calling his phone again. No answer. I hang up and send him a text instead.

I know what a hypocrite this makes me, but I'm worried about him. If he wasn't with me at the summerhouse and he's not at the renovation house, where the heck is he and who is he with? I start to panic and try to convince myself that he's fine. I curse myself for disappearing all the time, knowing that Jase must feel this way constantly. Guilt courses through me, a reminder that I don't quite deserve him.

I start walking back in the direction of town with a strange sense of dread that I just can't shake.

# 22 - Jase

I can feel the sun on my face, but I don't want to open my eyes. My head is pounding, and I feel my pulse throbbing in my neck and fingers. I instinctively reach out for Ayla and almost fall onto the floor. My eyes snap open and I have no idea where I am. The room is blindingly bright, so I cover both eyes with my hands.

I wish my head would stop pounding so I can think.

*Where the hell am I?*

I hear a noise behind me and sit up straight. I notice my shirt thrown over the back of the couch and grab for it quickly to pull it on. The sudden movement only makes my head pound faster and I can feel my heartbeat in my ears.

There's movement down the hall as I stand up and walk into the kitchen looking for water. I find a clean glass in one of the cabinets, fill it from the sink and quickly devour it before pouring another. My tongue is thick and dry, and the water does nothing to quench my thirst.

*I haven't been drunk like that in a long time. Now, I remember why.*

As I'm pouring the third glass of water, Jayde walks into the kitchen in a long t-shirt and nothing else. Her eyes have dark circles of makeup underneath them. She looks like I feel. I turn around without saying a word, find another glass and fill it with water before handing it to her. She smiles at me gratefully and grabs for it.

"Thanks," she mumbles after she drinks almost half the water in one gulp.

She doesn't seem to be embarrassed wearing only a t-shirt in front of me, but I avoid looking at her directly anyway. She leans against the counter next to me and her arm brushes my side.

There are a few moments of awkward silence as I try to think of something to say. I remember stopping at the pub last night. I remember the beer and the shots of tequila — the many, many shots of tequila. My stomach lurches and for a moment I think the water is going to come right back up, but it subsides. Chris walks into the kitchen without saying a word, sits at the counter and places his head in his hands.

"How much did we drink last night?" he croaks from under them.

Flashes of memory from last night come and go in a haze as I try to finish the water in my glass.

*My fight with Ayla earlier in the night …*

*Jayde with her hand on my arm and inching closer with every shot we finish …*

*Chris reliving high school life …*

*Jayde whispering in my ear …*

*Leaving my truck parked outside the bar to come here …*

*Chris making us drink more shots at his place …*

*Jayde using every opportunity to brush her hand on my arm, knee and back …*

*Me letting her …*

I groan out loud without intending to and both Chris and Jayde glance at me.

"Dude, I know," Chris says shaking his head at me. "What time is it?"

All three of us look at the clock on the microwave at the same time. It's after eleven. Guilt now courses through me in strong waves.

*A is probably wondering where the hell I am.*

The still angry part of me thinks that maybe she'll get a small taste of her own medicine, but my heart twists at the thought of her going to bed without me, angry and alone. I glance back at Jayde standing next to me. She catches my gaze and leans toward me, but I back away. She smells of stale beer and cigarettes. The water — and tequila — in my stomach once again threatens to rise up.

*I need to get out of this kitchen right now.*

*I need to get out of this apartment right now.*

I walk quickly to the couch to find my boots. As I sit down to put them on, I catch Chris walk into the kitchen out of the corner of my eye. He walks to Jayde, puts his arm around her and tries to kiss the side of her head, but she pulls away and scowls at him.

I hop up and start walking to the front door.

"Wait!"

Jayde's voice rings out across the apartment as I reach for the doorknob, stopping me in my tracks.

"His phone," she says, turning to Chris.

Chris nods and disappears down the hallway, leaving me alone with Jayde again. She walks around the living room, picking up cups and a blanket. As she bends over, a bright pink thong peeks out from under her t-shirt.

*I. Have. To. Get. Out. Of. Here.*

"Where is it?" Chris yells from down the hallway.

"Somewhere in the bedroom. On the dresser, I think," Jayde yells back.

She walks to me and when she is closer than I'm comfortable with, she speaks softly so only I can hear her.

"Like the show?"

She grins at me, dark circles of makeup and all.

*Where the hell is Chris with my phone?*

As I consider abandoning it here and getting a new one, a memory from last night flashes through my mind.

*The room is spinning and I want to fall asleep. My eyes are heavy, but I want to call A before I close them. We never go to bed angry with each other. That's my rule, but I can't find my phone anywhere. Jayde places a hand on my thigh. I should move it, but my arms feel fuzzy. I wish the room would stop spinning. Chris is sitting on the other side of Jayde. He leans in to kiss her and she kisses him back, but her hand moves farther up my thigh. I jolt upright, making the room spin even faster. Jayde tries to pull me toward her, but I push her hand away and stand up. Chris wraps his arms around Jayde and carries her down the hallway to his room. The door closes softly behind them and I'm alone in the dark living room. My heart is pounding and my mouth is dry. I stumble around the room looking for my phone, but I can't find it anywhere. I finally give up and fall back on the couch. I lay down, keeping one foot on the floor because that seems to slow the spinning room a bit.*

Jayde takes a step closer to me and places her hand on my chest. I grab it with my own to stop her.

"You and Chris—" I start to say, but she interrupts me.

"Oh, please. We get drunk. We hook up. So what? He's not my boyfriend. Besides, he's not quite you, is he? Why don't you take me for some breakfast?"

I drop her hand as Chris walks into the room with my phone.

"Who's A?"

"What?"

The sound of her nickname in the air here sounds out of place. All of my anger from last night disappears and all I can think about is going to see her. I want to be with her right now and I definitely don't want to be here any longer.

"You missed a few calls from A and a text."

Chris gives me the phone and my hand is already turning the doorknob.

"Jase, you don't have a car here remember?" Chris says, reaching out for Jayde as she steps closer to me.

"My car is here. I can bring him home," Jayde replies quickly and turns around. "Let me get dressed."

Chris starts to say something about breakfast to Jayde, but she rolls her eyes at him.

"I'm going to walk," I say to no one in particular as I walk out the front door.

Neither one of them has time to protest or even say goodbye, because I jog down the steps and out the front door of the apartment building without so much as a glance backward.

I look down at my phone to see three missed calls from A, one missed call from Ryan and a text message.

*Hey, babe. Sorry about last night. Call me when you get this. Miss you.*

*PS I went for a run this morning and saw your truck downtown. Found the keys and brought it to the reno house for you. You ok?*

I immediately make a phone call, wishing once again that I had gone straight home last night. It only rings once.

"Pop? I need you to come get me. No questions and no judgments, but I need you to come right now. And bring aspirin — like a lifetime supply of it."

# 23 - Ayla

I check my phone again. Not one missed call. No texts back from Jase. I ask Ryan to call him when I get back to the house from my run, just in case he isn't answering because he's still mad at me. Ryan gets his voicemail, too. He gives me a pointed look when I sigh in frustration as I hear Jase's voicemail pick up.

"Yeah, I know. I recognize the irony here, Ry. You think he's trying to prove a point?" I ask while biting my thumbnail nervously. "I mean, he's fine, right? I shouldn't worry or anything, because Jase is always fine, right?"

I begin to pace back and forth in front of Ryan as he tries to hide his grin. I reach out and slap him on the arm playfully.

"This isn't funny!"

Ryan reaches out as I walk in front of him again and pulls me to the couch next to him.

"Stop pacing. You're driving me crazy. I'm sure Jase is perfectly fine. Sounds to me like he had a little too much to drink last night and is probably sleeping it off."

"Yeah, but where? If he's not here or at the reno house, where would he be?"

I give up on my nails and absentmindedly chew on my lower lip.

"Maybe he's at his dad's house or in one of the bungalows with the guys. A, he's fine. Will you relax?"

Ryan grabs for my hand and squeezes it, smiling at me. I flush, slightly embarrassed for being so worried.

"You're right. Can we not tell him I did this, please? He will never let me forget it," I say with a smile.

"It'll be our little secret, but you're cute when you're nervous, A."

Ryan reaches out and pinches my cheek before I push him away. He pulls me into a hug.

"Glad to see you smiling. I miss it."

I squeeze him tighter before letting him go and pull him to his feet as I get up from the couch. I hear laughter and voices on the back deck, so we both head in that direction. Ryan walks out the sliding door as I head to the fridge. It's just about time for lunch, but I'm not hungry. I reach for a beer instead. Placing it on the counter, I see Ashleigh wrap her arms around Ryan on the back deck. She is standing next to a green-eyed brunette and I watch as Ryan says hello to her. The three of them continue to have a conversation that I can't hear as I open the beer and drink half of it quickly. The familiar taste seems to calm my nerves and I finish the second half just as fast. I grab a second from the fridge as Jesse walks into the kitchen.

"Since when do you come in the front?" I ask him, offering him the newly opened beer.

He grabs for it and takes a swig before handing it back to me.

"I saw Ashleigh and her friend on the back deck with Ry and figured I'd avoid having to talk to them," Jesse says with a grin.

I laugh out loud.

"Who's the brunette? I don't think I've met her yet," Jesse says raising his eyebrows up and down.

I shrug and swallow another gulp of beer, handing it back to Jesse.

"Not sure. I haven't either. I was on my way out there but thought drinking alone in the kitchen sounded like more fun."

Jesse's grin widens as he finishes the beer.

We hear high-pitched laughter through the glass and something about the sound annoys me. I look out at Ryan and see Ashleigh on his lap with the new girl sitting close to Ryan, her hand on his arm. Surprisingly, Ashleigh doesn't seem to notice. Ryan catches my eye and waves us out onto the deck to join them. I hear Jesse groan behind me.

"Guess we should go out there," I say, wishing we didn't have to.

"Another beer?" I ask Jesse as I reach into the fridge.

"Definitely. Maybe make it two," he says as I hand a cold one to him.

I grab as many as I can carry as Jesse laughs.

"Just in case," I say as I wink at him before heading out the sliding glass door to the deck, more obnoxious laughter filling the air as I do.

All three of them stop laughing as I step out on to the deck, carefully balancing the armful of beer bottles. Ashleigh raises her eyebrows at me but says nothing. I sit down across from them at the table and line up the bottles in front of me. Jesse sits next to me after slapping Ryan on the back to say hello.

"And who are you?" Ashleigh's friend says to Jesse, ignoring me altogether.

"I'm Jesse," he says reaching out a hand as she shakes it.

Her green eyes sparkle in the sun as Jesse's handshake lingers. He wears a goofy grin that makes me roll my eyes and elbow him in the side. He quickly pulls his hand back and returns it to his beer.

"I'm Ashleigh's friend, Jayde," Green Eyes says.

She reaches for one of the bottles on the table.

"Mind if I have one?" she asks, when it's already open and in her hands.

She takes a long, slow sip, her eyes never leaving Jesse's. She licks her lips when she finishes like she's in a damn porno.

*Seriously?*

I fight the urge to take the beer back from her, so I don't have to witness that again.

*I never have been good at sharing.*

"I'm Ayla," I say to Jayde, not offering her my hand on purpose as I finish my beer and open another one.

I manage a tight grin as she flashes me a wide smile. Jayde brings the bottle to her mouth again as I cringe.

"How's your day going, Ash?" I ask her, trying to change the focus at the table.

"Pretty good," Ashleigh says, rubbing Ryan's back slowly.

"You two are so darn cute," Jayde gushes at the two of them before Ashleigh can say anything more.

Ashleigh beams as Ryan shifts in his seat to pull her closer. It makes me think of Jase and I reach for my phone to text him again as Ashleigh and Jayde continue talking.

*Just want to be sure ur still alive. U ok?*

I leave the phone in my lap as Jesse opens another beer and offers it to me. I take the first sip and hand it back to him so we can share it.

"You wouldn't believe who I hung out with last night," I hear Jayde say. "I stayed behind at Chris' bar after you girls left and had a few drinks waiting for him to get off of work—"

"Ugh, why do you continue to hang out with him?" Ashleigh asks her.

I take the beer back from Jesse's hand and drain it halfway, trying to tune them out as Jayde explains that hanging out with Chris has its benefits including late night hookups and free drinks.

My phone buzzes in my lap and I look down to see that Jase responded.

*So sorry. Late night. Miss u tho. I'll be over shortly.*

"What are you smiling about?" Jesse whispers in my ear.

I hand the beer back to him and show him the phone.

"Oh, so you two are talking again I take it," he says with a grin.

I shrug at Jesse as Jayde continues her story about last night.

"Anyway, I may not be hanging out with Chris for much longer, because I have my eye on someone else now."

"Oh, thank God," Ashleigh says laughing as I watch Jesse slump in his seat a bit.

"Yeah, and I was hoping you and Ryan could hook a girl up. We hit it off last night, had a few drinks and ended up spending the night together."

"That's nothing new," I hear Ryan say under his breath.

Ashleigh pinches him underneath the table, but Jayde continues, pretending not to hear him. I stifle a laugh as I try to catch Ryan's eye.

"I took his phone last night so I could save my number in it and may have taken a few pictures with it," Jayde says as I scrunch my face in disgust.

My phone buzzes in my lap with another text from Jase.

*On my way — can we talk?*

"Oh, you're bad!" Ashleigh slaps at her playfully. "So, who is this guy of yours?"

"Ryan's friend, Jase. Can you hook us up?"

Ashleigh's face drains of all color as Ryan takes a sharp breath in.

"Oh, shit," I hear Jesse say next to me.

"What did you just say?" I spit out at her, willing her to spontaneously burst into flames where she sits.

"A, take a breath—" Ryan says, standing up and almost dumping Ashleigh on the floor in the process.

Adrenaline is coursing through my veins, but I can't will my legs to move.

"You're A?" Jayde says to me as if I don't quite measure up to the name. "You called him a few times this morning, right? We were a little busy when you called."

She smiles at me with an evil that seeps out between every perfect tooth in her mouth.

I want to bounce her face off the table in front of her, my rage boiling over and making me shake, but as I stand up both Jesse and Ryan block her from my view. My hands are balled into tiny fists at my side as I look into Jesse's eyes, pleading with him to move.

Before he can answer, the back door slides open and closes as we all spin around. I catch a glimpse of Jase before the edges of my vision gets fuzzy and then the whole world fades to black.

# 24 - Jase

My head is still pounding and no amount of aspirin seems to make it go away. Thankfully, dad picks me up without asking a single question. He takes me to his house to make a greasy breakfast and we eat mostly in silence with dad asking a few questions about the fellowship here and there. I take a shower and get dressed slowly, all the while thinking about A. I feel guilty that I let some other girl — a girl I barely know — flirt with me all night. I think a part of me enjoyed it, too. I keep telling myself it was the alcohol, but I'm not sure.

I would never cheat on A, but I let things get out of hand last night. It was nice to forget about all of the frustration and fighting and helplessness I feel with A lately and just have fun. This morning, I regret it. I want to erase all of it. I want to forget about Jayde and her soft touches. I want to forget about my fight with A last night and pretend it never happened. I want to forget last night happened altogether. Mostly, I want to forget about the tequila. I vow to never drink again as I fight another surge of nausea.

I pick up my phone as it vibrates in my hand. It's a text from A.

*Just want to be sure ur still alive. U ok?*

I instantly wish she was here with me so I can kiss her. I have to tell her what happened, but everything in me is dreading it. I quickly finish getting dressed.

I look in the mirror, staring at my reflection. I look like hell, but I feel worse. I text A quickly.

*So sorry. Late night. Miss u tho. I'll be over shortly.*

I want to tell her that I love her, but it feels like a crappy thing to do before I tell her where I was last night. I ask dad to drop me off at the renovation house so I can get my truck. I find the keys where A left them behind the visor. I smile to myself as I start the truck, her perfume still lingering in the cab. I text her again when I'm a few minutes away.

*On my way — can we talk?*

She still hasn't responded when I pull into the driveway at the summerhouse. I walk in the front door and call for her but hear voices on the back deck, so I walk through the kitchen to the back door. I catch a glimpse of Jayde at the table with Ashleigh as my heart jumps.

*What the hell is she doing here?!*

I watch as A jumps to her feet across the table from Jayde, but Ryan and Jesse are in front of her as she does.

*Shit.*

I open and close the sliding door quickly, stepping out onto the deck and stopping the commotion momentarily. Ryan's eyes are full of anger as he glances at me, but Jesse's are wide in surprise. Ayla stares at me for a moment, her eyes full of an emotion that I can't quite make out, before her legs buckle and she passes out.

Jesse catches her in his arms before she hits the deck, and I am by her side in seconds. Panic fills my throat as I grab her from him, yelling her name over and over. Ryan rushes to the other side of her.

"Let's get some water for her face," he yells to Ashleigh and they both disappear inside.

Jayde is out of her seat but doesn't move from where she stands.

I watch as A's pupils move back and forth under her eyelids before they flutter open. She locks eyes with me and relief floods my body before her eyes fill with a hurt like I've never seen there before. She pushes away from me, stumbling to her feet and reaches out for Jesse. He grabs her arm to steady her.

"You okay, A?" he asks, looking terrified.

"I'm fine, Jess. I'm just great."

The color is returning to her cheeks, but it does nothing to hide the hurt from her face. It makes my own heart break. She straightens herself, standing on her own now as Ryan and Ashleigh run out the back door.

"A, what the hell happened?"

Ryan rushes toward her.

"Nothing, I'm fine. My heart rate gets too high and I pass out. It's happened a few times before. I'm fine now."

She turns away from him, walking toward the house with Jesse following her. I reach out for her as she walks by me, but she shoves my arm aside.

"Don't touch me!"

I jump at the sound of her voice, but she continues by me without noticing.

"A, come on. Talk to me," I plead with her as she reaches for the sliding door. "Please. I can explain."

I take two steps toward her, but the look on her face makes me stop again.

"Oh, Jayde explained enough already."

I turn toward Jayde in confusion, still unsure of why she is here in the first place. When I turn back towards A, she is disappearing inside. I look at Jesse as his mouth opens and closes like he wants to say something. Instead, he shoves his hands in both pockets and follows quickly after Ayla.

I rub my temples, my pulse now pounding stronger than ever. I look at Ryan through my hands, but he looks at me with disgust.

"Ry, it was just a few drinks—" I begin to say, but Ryan doesn't let me finish.

"You're joking, right?" Ryan says as he takes a step toward me.

Ashleigh stands between us, but she won't meet my eyes.

"Where were you last night, Jase? Better yet, where were you this morning?"

I don't answer, but he can see the guilt in my eyes.

"With her of all people?!" Ryan says loudly, pointing at Jayde with the same look of disgust.

"Hold on–" Jayde starts to say, but Ryan holds both hands in the air to stop her from saying another word.

"Don't. You've said enough."

He turns and walks inside the house, slamming the sliding door behind him. Ashleigh follows him, quietly opening and closing the sliding door without a sound.

Shock locks my feet in place. I let out a long breath, one I had been holding in without realizing. I shake my head and close my eyes, trying to clear the look in A's eyes when she stared back at me. I open my eyes again to find Jayde still there. I'm not sure why, but I half expected her to disappear.

*Wishful thinking?*

She takes a few steps toward me. Her green eyes are wide with concern and she reaches out for my arm. My entire body pulls away from her and the hurt in her eyes radiates out through her face.

"You didn't do anything wrong, Jase," she says quietly. "I don't know why everyone overreacted. I was only asking Ryan and Ash to set us up. I mentioned that we had a good time last night and that I really liked you, and then all hell broke loose. I didn't realize that the girl sitting across from me was the A that called you this morning. She's not quite what I pictured in my head."

Jayde scrunches her nose and pauses for a moment before speaking again.

"She sure knows how to make a scene, doesn't she?"

*She definitely does.*

I think this to myself but won't admit it to Jayde.

"Ayla is my girlfriend, Jayde. We've been together for a long time," I say quietly, trying not to take my frustration out on her even though I can hear it in my voice.

"Oh," Jayde says, but she doesn't look apologetic at all.

She pauses for only a moment before smiling again.

"Well, you weren't thinking too much about your girlfriend last night, were you?"

I want to deny it, but a part of me knows there is some truth to what she says. If I were thinking about A, I wouldn't have ended up at Chris' apartment last night, whether I had been drinking or not. I wouldn't have flirted with Jayde at the bar or given her the wrong idea. I really wish I had gone straight home last night.

"I think I really screwed up," I say out loud without meaning to.

I start to pace slowly back and forth on the deck, lost in thought and momentarily forgetting Jayde is there.

I look through the sliding door into the house and wonder if A is still here. Knowing her, she probably took off with Jesse somewhere. The thought of Jesse comforting her from big, bad Jase makes me clench my jaw in anger. The throbbing in my temples increases and I find myself sitting at the picnic table. I don't even remember sitting down. Jayde is sitting across from me. I can feel her gaze on me, but I refuse to look up.

"Do you want to go somewhere and talk, Jase?" Jayde asks, trying to catch my eye.

"I need to find A, Jayde. I should talk to her, apologize to her and beg for forgiveness or something."

My hands find their way to the top of my head. I know that I won't be doing any of those things until A is ready to hear what I have to say. She is so damn stubborn, and even though she has a right to be angry with me, I wish she'd given me a chance to explain what happened. But I know her well enough to know that isn't going to happen until she is good and ready to listen. Until then, I have to sit around and feel guilty, I guess.

"Let's go grab something to eat. It'll take your mind off of everything for a little bit and give her a chance to cool down."

Jayde moves next to me and reaches for my arm and her soft touch brings back everything from the night before. I jump up from where I'm sitting.

"No, Jayde, no. That's not a good idea."

I begin to walk toward the stairs and head to my truck, but Jayde stands in my way. She puts her hands on my chest to stop me but lets them linger there for longer than I'm comfortable with.

"What else are you going to do, Jase? She's mad at you. Ryan is mad, although I'm not sure why. That other kid who follows A around like a puppy dog seemed like he wasn't sure if he should be mad or not … "

I laugh out loud at Jayde and her grin widens.

"That's Jesse," I tell her, politely removing her hands from my chest and returning them to her sides. "He does kind of follow her around like a puppy dog, doesn't he?"

"I only just met them and I can already see that. It's a little hypocritical for her to get mad at you for hanging out with me but then immediately leave with him. We can be friends, Jase. There's no harm in that," she says with a wink. "Besides, she's already mad at you. What's the worst that can happen? She'll be twice as mad?"

Everything in my head and my heart is screaming at me to run to the truck and never look back. I know hanging out with Jayde is a horrible idea. It'll only make things worse between me and Ayla, but Jayde has a point. It's nice to have someone see things from my perspective for once. I'm not doing anything different than Ayla is when she hangs out with Jesse. Ayla was angry with me last night when I was jealous of Jesse, but then flipped out today about Jayde without even giving me a chance to explain.

*Talk about a double standard.*

I don't know what Jayde said to Ayla or what she implied happened between us, but the truth is that nothing did happen. I don't have any interest in playing games, but maybe A will have a better understanding of how her relationship with Jesse makes me feel now.

I finally look into Jayde's green eyes, knowing that the little voice in my head is right.

*This is a bad idea.*

# 25 - Ayla

I am so hurt and angry that I can't see straight. Tears are streaming down my cheeks and I angrily swipe them away with the back of my hands.

*I hate her.*

I didn't like her from the first moment I met her. Then to find out that she's who Jase was with all night last night.

*And this morning, too.*

I grind my teeth back and forth as I slam the large gate open. Metal clashes against metal and the sound echoes loudly enough to make me pause.

"Sorry," I mumble out loud to no one in particular.

All else in the cemetery is quiet, with the exception of my apology hanging in the air. I let my anger disturb the peace here and I mentally lecture myself to calm down.

"Hey," a voice says softly behind me.

I jump in the air at the sound and spin around to find Jesse, nervously shifting from foot to foot.

"Jesse! I didn't know you followed me," I say, embarrassed that there are still remnants of tears clinging to my cheeks. "You didn't have to. I mean, thanks, I guess."

I sniff as Jesse laughs.

"I followed you to make sure you are okay. That was craziness back there," he says looking at me, then quickly looks beyond me and up the hill to where Tate's headstone is. "I don't even know what to say, A."

"There's nothing to say, Jess. All I can think about is punching her in the face."

Jesse laughs, which manages to make me smile, too. He very slowly reaches out a hand and lightly brushes my cheek with his thumb, removing any evidence of tears. When he pulls his hand away, he reaches into his pocket to produce a flask stashed there.

"What would I do without you, Jesse?" I say to him, grabbing the flask and putting it to my lips without even asking what is in it.

I start to head up the hill with Jesse, handing him the flask as we walk. I cough as the liquid burns its way to my belly. It sits there like the fiery ball of fury burning inside me. We reach Tate's headstone and both sit down in the grass at the same time in silence. Jesse nods as if Tate is standing in front of him and starts to pour whiskey into the grass in front of us.

I grab the flask from his hand quickly before it spills more than a few drops.

"You know Tate of all people would not want you wasting that!" I say to Jesse, smiling.

"This is very true," Jesse says, nodding to an invisible Tate. "She's still keeping us all in line, Tate. We sure do miss you, though. It's not quite the same around here without you."

I bite the inside of my cheek to keep any additional tears at bay.

"Tate-I-Am, you have to hear what happened today … "

I proceed to tell Tate about Jase disappearing all night and then meeting Jayde this morning. Jesse chimes in here and there, but mostly I talk to Tate as Jesse listens.

We both take turns drinking from the flask and the memories of the three of us doing this while Tate was alive consume me. The three of us were the youngest of the group and we were constantly left to fend for ourselves when the rest of the guys went out. I lose my train of thought and pause in the middle of a sentence, staring at Jesse with a smile.

"What?" he asks me, raising an eyebrow in question.

"I miss this, you know?"

The emotion that takes over Jesse's face engulfs his features, drowning his eyes in it. I recognize it immediately because it is exactly how I feel every time I think about Tate. I reach out and take his hand. We sit like this for a long time, both of us afraid to break the silence or meet each other's eyes. This is where Tate would chime in and say something funny to make us both laugh. This time the silence continues, though, because Tate was taken from us and neither one of us have any idea how to deal with it.

# 26 - Jase

I try calling her again, but after a few rings the call goes directly to her voicemail. I grit my teeth in frustration. I try texting her again, but she hasn't responded to the last three, so I don't have much hope for an answer to this one.

*Can we pls talk? I know ur mad, but nothing happened. Call me? I can come over if ur home?*

I hit send, my thumb pausing over the button for a moment before I do. I wait a moment and see that she is reading it, but her silence continues.

I look out the window at the water, watching the boats bob up and down in unison. The sun is setting, encasing everything in an orange-pink glow. A hasn't responded to a single text or phone call all day and my frustration is growing as the minutes tick by.

Jayde abruptly flops into her seat across from me and I quickly shuffle the phone into my pocket.

"Sorry, there was a line for the bathroom," she says, smiling apologetically into her wine glass.

There's a thin line of purple marking her face on either side of her mouth, making her look like a female version of the joker. If it had been A across from me, I'd smile and wipe it off for her and she'd probably laugh at me. But with Jayde, something about the wine on her face disgusts me. We've been sitting at the same table all afternoon and Jayde has yet to manage taking a sip without the marks appearing. It makes her look sinister and the later in the day it gets, the darker the lines appear.

*Didn't she notice that when she was in the bathroom?*

I mentioned it to her only once, during her first glass of wine, but didn't have the heart to tell her it was still there after she swiped at both sides of her mouth.

"So, now what?" Jayde says, placing the now-empty wine glass on the table with a loud clatter.

A few people around us glance our way with raised eyebrows. I lean in towards her to keep my voice low.

"Now is probably a good time for me to take you home, Jayde."

As the day has gone on, my frustration with Jayde has grown as well. With every drink she has, with every word she says — it all reminds me how much she isn't Ayla. I pull my phone out of my pocket and glance at it under the table. The blank screen alerts me that I have no new calls or text messages. Jayde reaches out while I'm doing so and places her hand against my cheek.

"Such a sad face, Jase," Jayde giggles. "Turn that frown upside down."

She looks into my eyes searching for something, but I have no idea what.

I take my hand and place it over hers on my cheek before removing it to the table. I do everything very slowly, as if I'm dealing with a child whose feelings I don't want to hurt.

I walk over to the bar and pay our tab. While I'm waiting for them to run the credit card, I can feel someone staring at me. I look up and lock eyes with Jake, who is sitting at a table near the bar with a group of people I don't recognize.

Jake is a friend of Ayla's and a friend of mine through extension. Jake and Tate dated in secret for a few years before Tate was killed and Ayla was one of very few people that knew. After Tate passed away, a lot of us tried to reach out to Jake, but he pulled away from all of us. Some of the guys weren't too kind to Jake when Tate was alive, so I think it is hard for him to forgive that even after Tate's death. Ayla will hear from him from time to time, but I think it's hard for both of them to be together without Tate around.

I smile at Jake and wave. He waves back, but then quickly returns his attention to the people at his table, so I walk back to mine.

"Ready?" I say to Jayde.

She stands up, stumbling a bit and reaches for my arm to steady herself. I walk her through the bar area and outside into the warm night air. After getting her into the truck I realize that I have no idea where she lives.

"What direction am I heading, Jayde?"

I look at her and she bats her long eyelashes at me with a smile. I turn and look out my window instead.

*This was a bad idea.*

While I spent the afternoon nursing two beers and constantly checking my phone, Jayde sat across from me trying to convince me not to worry about A and downing glass after glass of red wine.

"We could go to your place?" Jayde says, miraculously managing to not slur any of her words.

"Jayde, I don't know how else to say this or how to make it more clear for you. I'm with Ayla. I'm taking you home. Now."

I've tried to be patient and polite, but my frustration has reached a boiling point. I know that it's not all Jayde's fault that we were together last night. I could have easily done a million things that would have ended the night differently. I know that it's not her fault that she accidentally told A before I had the chance to. I'm trying not to hold any of that against her, but I'm starting to get the feeling that being polite to her is only going to mean more trouble for me and I'm in enough already.

Jayde pushes herself with some effort into the middle seat in the truck. Our legs are now touching and when I glance down, she grabs for my hand and places it high up on her thigh. I pull away from her, but she pulls back on my arm in a small tug of war.

"It can be our little secret, Jase. I'm really good at keeping secrets."

I pull my arm out of her grasp completely, shaking my head.

"I don't know why I have to keep repeating this, but nothing is going to happen between us. Not now. Not ever."

"Forever is a long time, Jase," she says with a teasing smirk. "Give me some time."

Jayde scoots back to the passenger side of the truck as I stare at her like she's lost her mind. She catches my eye and crosses her arms over her chest, her mood instantly changing.

"I'm basically throwing myself at you and you're still worried about your girlfriend who isn't currently speaking to you? I don't get it. I really don't. You'll regret this, Jase. I promise you that."

I don't feel the need to defend A or our relationship to Jayde. Currently, the only things I regret include hanging out with Jayde. I let silence hang in the air instead.

"Where am I dropping you off?" I say as calmly as I can manage.

"Bring me to Ashleigh's," Jayde replies without glancing at me.

Even though she is angry with me, I feel relieved now that she is sitting on the opposite side of the truck staring out the window. She doesn't say a single word until I stop in front of Ashleigh's house. I notice Ryan's car parked out front and pause for a moment, trying to decide whether or not I should go in to talk to him.

"This isn't over, Jase. Not by a long shot. There's a connection here whether you want to admit it or not, and I'm going to make you see how perfect we could be together."

Jayde smiles widely at me, the marks from the wine almost disappearing into dimples on either side of her mouth.

*She doesn't just look crazy. I think she may actually be crazy.*

I don't have anything left to say to her, so I jump out of the truck and head to the front door without responding. I knock twice quickly and one of Ashleigh's roommates answers the door.

"I'm Ryan's friend, Jase. Is he here?"

The blonde in front of me snaps her gum, looking bored.

"He's around back on the deck. You can come through this way."

She steps aside to let me pass. As she does, she notices Jayde walking up the sidewalk behind me.

"Hey Jayde," the blonde replies, the bubble gum in her mouth snapping loudly. "C'mon in, girl!"

I leave the two at the door to continue their conversation and walk through the house out onto the back deck. Ashleigh and Ryan are seated at a wrought iron table with a few other people. Ashleigh introduces me quickly before I ask Ryan if I can speak to him for a minute. He nods, gets up and motions for me to follow him down toward the water and away from everyone else.

"What is going on, Jase?" Ryan asks before we've fully stopped walking.

"Nothing, Ry. I wish I had the chance to talk to Ayla myself before Jayde said something. You want the truth? I went to see Chris at his bar downtown. I had a few drinks and he introduced me to Jayde. After the bar closed, Chris invited me and Jayde back to his place. I drank too much to drive, so I slept it off on his couch while Chris and Jayde spent the night together in his room. End of story."

Ryan lets out a long whistle.

"Well, that's not how Jayde made it sound at all. Whether she knows Ayla is your girlfriend or not, she made it sound like the two of you really hit it off last night. She was asking Ash to hook you two up and that's when A lost it."

Ryan puts a hand on my shoulder and squeezes.

"I'm sorry I didn't give you the benefit of the doubt, man. You're like my brother," he says, his voice so thick with emotion that I can't meet his eyes.

"Sometimes I get so caught up in worrying about her that I forget to be your best friend, too."

Ryan looks at me apologetically and offers me a handshake. I grip his hand tightly and pull him into a brief hug.

"I know you worry about her like I do, Ry, but I need your help now. I can't get A to respond to me, but I need her to know that nothing happened between Jayde and me. Yes, I'm frustrated, and yes, things haven't been easy between us lately, but I would never do anything to hurt her. Ever."

Ryan nods at me.

"I know that, and A does, too. She got caught up in the heat of the moment like I did. Jayde made it sound way worse than it is and Ayla got jealous and angry. She's had all day to cool off. Let's head back to the house. She'll end up there eventually if she isn't back already."

Ryan yells up to Ashleigh on the deck that he's heading back to the summerhouse with me and she nods. As Ryan and I stare up at the deck, Jayde's face appears next to Ashleigh's. She waves at me and blows me a kiss.

I roll my eyes at Ryan and motion to him to start walking to our vehicles.

"That one is trouble, Jase," Ryan says to me with raised eyebrows.

"You have no idea how much," I say to Ryan, keeping my eyes on the ground.

# 27 - Ayla

After the cemetery, Jesse and I head back to the summerhouse. Thankfully, Jase and Jayde are nowhere in sight. Jesse heads off to his bungalow to take a nap. I head inside to do the same, but as I'm walking through the front door, I hear my phone vibrating on the wood floor of the living room. I remember throwing it there in a rage as I bolted out of the house earlier.

Shaking my head at myself, I pick up the phone. Thankfully, the screen is still intact. Three missed calls, all from Jase, and three text messages. The most recent one came in a moment ago.

*Can we pls talk? I know ur mad, but nothing happened. Call me? I can come over if ur home?*

Guilt courses through me, but I'm still not sure what to say to Jase. Just the thought of Jayde sitting across from me at the table earlier, bubbling and gushing about the new guy she hit it off with makes me spill over with rage. The anger rushes me all over again.

Do I really think Jase cheated on me? No. I can't picture Jase ever cheating, even with someone who looks like Jayde. I just can't get over that he spent an entire night with another girl without calling or texting me. I feel betrayed by my best friend. I hate that he went running off from an argument with me and hung out with another girl instead. And part of me worries that if things like this happen when I'm only a few miles away, what happens the rest of the year when I'm in New York? Worse yet, what will happen when he spends an entire summer in California for the fellowship next year?

I walk to the kitchen and open a bottle of water trying to clear my head as I place my phone on the counter next to the fridge. Before I finish the last of the water, the phone vibrates again.

I sigh in frustration, but when I pick up the phone, I see the text message isn't from Jase, but from Jake. I used to hang out with Jake and Tate almost every day, but after Tate died it became very difficult for both of us to hang out with each other. I think we remind the other of Tate's absence and we slowly drifted apart because of it. We talk on the phone every now and then, but it's rare that we hang out anymore which is why his text message surprises me so much.

*A – we should meet up to chat. Miss you!*

Without thinking too much about it, I call Jake immediately. He answers on the first ring. His voice is loud and clear, but there's a lot of background noise and I can tell he's with a group of people.

"Is this a bad time? I got your text and was surprised to hear from you. Is everything okay?"

I can sense Jake's smile through the phone.

"I miss your voice, kiddo. I'm leaving dinner with some friends. Everything's fine, but do you want to meet me at the old house in fifteen minutes? We can play cards like the old days?"

"I'll bring the cookies," I say to Jake after agreeing to meet him and then we hang up.

I grab a Tupperware container of chocolate chip cookies I made a few days ago. They don't taste anywhere near as good as Cora's cookies, but I'm sure Jake will love them anyway. Cora is the Gematti's in-house chef who was extremely close with Tate. Cora always made chocolate chip cookies for Jake, among many other things, and continues to bring him food to this day.

I decide to walk to Jake's old house with the cookies in hand, not wanting to wake Jesse to drive me or borrow his keys. I'm curious what brought on Jake's sudden urge to hang out, but I'm happy that he called. I could use an extra friend today.

I'm more surprised that Jake asked me to come to this house. He used to live here with his mother but moved into an apartment with a bunch of friends last year. His mother still lives in the house, but Jake doesn't go there as much. Jake's mother is an alcoholic — something Jake has never kept hidden. He's been through a lot with her and always felt like he had to take care of her. After Tate was killed, Jake decided it was time to move out. I think being in that house reminded him of the time he spent there with Tate and it all became too much. Because Tate kept their entire relationship hidden from most people including Ryan and Mr. Gematti, Tate and Jake spent most of their time together at Jake's house. Jake has not had an easy life, probably even more so than I realize, but he hates pity almost as much as I do so we don't talk much about his mother or Tate anymore. He used to try and ask me a million questions about the night that Tate died, but I couldn't ever find the words to answer and eventually he gave up. I finally gave up asking how his mother is, too.

When Jake's house is in view, I see that he is already parked in the driveway and waiting for me at the front door. I smile and wave at him, willing my legs to move faster.

When I get a little closer, I see Jake's face and notice there's something in his expression that makes me uneasy. I begin to realize that this visit may not be all fun and games and catching up like I thought. He has something to tell me, and by the looks of it, he's worried about whatever it is.

# 28 - Jase

When Ryan and I get back to the summerhouse, it is empty and silent. A is nowhere to be found, but her perfume hangs in the air just like it did in the cab of my truck. I wonder if we just missed her.

Jesse's truck is in the driveway, so she's not with him unless they are down in his bungalow together. I feel the jealousy creep up at that thought, but I remind myself that I spent the better part of the day with Jayde.

I have a sick feeling in my stomach as I think about the things that Jayde said to me in the truck earlier. I'll admit that it's nice to have someone notice and pay attention to me. I didn't feel invisible today like I sometimes feel with A — not even once. It's not always like that with us, but A gets so wrapped up in her own head sometimes that I feel like she forgets I exist. Sitting across from Jayde and feeling her look at me — really look at me — felt good even though my mind was focused on A. I feel guilty thinking this, but it's true.

I keep asking myself why I let Jayde flirt with me last night and I think the simplest answer is that I was flattered by the attention. I didn't have to put any effort in. I didn't have to worry or stress or feel rejected. There's no history behind us making things complicated. It all was easy and so I let it happen. And if I'm being completely honest, I had fun.

The feeling in my stomach gets heavier, thick with churning nerves. Should I tell Ayla all this and risk making her angrier with me than she already is? I hate that she feels I was hiding something from her, but I also resent that she overreacts to every little thing. I wish she had given me a chance to explain, but her emotions are explosive. I always find myself trying to anticipate what is going to set her off next.

At the same time, I long for her when she's not with me. Every cell of my body needs her — wants her — aches for her. I feel like something is missing without her. I don't feel complete when she's not with me.

I look at my phone once more. The blank screen showing no response mocks me. I toss my phone on the table next to me as Ryan hands me a bottle of iced tea. We head out to the back deck, sitting down across from each other at the picnic table.

"You have to let her cool off. You know that better than anyone. She'll come back and she'll probably laugh about it with you when you tell her what a psycho Jayde is."

I grin and take a long gulp of the tea, letting the cold numb my insides.

"She's not psycho, Ry. She's … persistent."

Ryan laughs at me.

"You forget I didn't just meet her today. Her and Ash have been hanging out for a few weeks now. She's crazy, believe me."

I stay quiet, but I have the strange urge to defend Jayde even though I think Ryan may be right.

My phone buzzes from inside and I jump up to grab it. My heart drops when I realize it wasn't A texting me, but Jayde.

*thought u might need some cheering up*

The phone vibrates in my hand again and this time a picture pops up of Jayde in a very tiny bathing suit blowing a kiss to the camera.

*Persistent may have been an understatement.*

# 29 - Ayla

I'm sitting at the small table in Jake's kitchen alone. I swipe the trail of cookie crumbs that sit in front of me into my hand and drop it into the trash bag taped to the counter next to me.

Jake had just finished telling me about running into Jase and Jayde — I'm assuming Jayde by Jake's description of her — when we heard a loud noise down the hall and Jake went running to find his mom.

I help myself to another cookie and look around the bare kitchen. Being here brings back so many memories of Tate that it makes it hard to swallow what's left of the cookie in my mouth. If I listen hard enough, I can almost hear Tate's contagious laugh echo in the room. We spent many late nights in this kitchen playing cards and eating cookies. I gently place the half-eaten cookie back on the plate in front of me.

Jake walks into the kitchen with handfuls of white tissue covered in blood. I hop up from the chair.

*There's a lot of blood on those tissues.*

My mind begins to spin with images I fight every day to get away from.

"Is she okay?!"

Jake looks up and rolls his eyes at me as he stuffs the bloodied tissues into the trash bag.

"She's never okay, A. She needs to stop drinking, but she won't. She keeps getting a bloody nose, but insists she's fine and won't go see a doctor. And God forbid she goes a day without a drink. I need to get out of here."

Jake washes his hands while I stare wide eyed at the garbage bag where the tissues stay. I can see the blood through the white bag, and it makes my mind flash to memories of the night that Tate died. Jake follows my gaze and realizes that I'm in the throes of a flashback. It pulls me violently backwards when it happens, and

I'm reliving the entire night. I'm no longer in Jake's mother's kitchen. I'm back out on the road, that night two years ago. I'm trapped underneath strong arms that hold me while I have to watch as Tate dies, again.

Jake grabs my hand and pulls me out into the backyard. He places both arms on either side of my face and tells me to take deep breaths. I am breathing heavy and I don't hear him at first. His voice is confusing and doesn't make sense among the memories and voices I'm hearing. I can't seem to catch my breath and I feel like I may not ever be able to breathe again.

When my eyes finally focus again, Jake looks terrified.

"A, I'm so sorry. I didn't even think. Are you okay?!"

His eyes dance nervously over my face as I try to ground myself to the here and now. I blink, embarrassed even though I know I shouldn't be, especially in front of Jake. I take a few quick breaths of fresh air trying to erase what's left of the ugly memories from my mind. Jake pulls me to a swing where we both sit down as I continue to get my breathing under control. I look out into the sunflowers that surround the swing and try to blink away tears.

"A—" Jake says softly.

"I'm okay."

I smile weakly at Jake.

"It's crazy how some things trigger that. I have no control over it. I go immediately back to that night — like I'm living it all over again."

Jake nods and gives me a hug that I can't seem to find the energy to return. I'm still trying to gather myself back in the present and remember that everything with Tate was two years ago. It's not happening now, even though it feels as real as it does.

Jake waits awhile before saying anything, patient and calm. I let his calm wash over me, and I wish it wasn't so hard to spend time with him because I think his calm could help me.

"So, why the hell was Jase basically carrying some drunk girl out the door today?"

I laugh in spite of the churn in my stomach, knowing Jake is desperately trying to change the subject and get my mind focused on something else. That and Jake has always loved gossip. I look at him and shrug.

"Better yet, why was he with her at all? I thought she was a relative or something, but then I watched the way she was talking to him and reaching across the table at him. It was weird, A. Is something going on there? Are you two not together anymore? Tell me the details!"

A flash of anger spikes through my body at the thought of Jayde touching Jase, but I ignore the vibrations it sends through my limbs. I grind my teeth, trying to will the anger to subside. Once I find my voice, I proceed to tell Jake about the fellowship, about all of the fights with Jase lately including the one we had last night, about him leaving and disappearing all night, and then meeting Jayde and finding out that they spent the night together. I tell him that Jase has been trying to get ahold of me all day to talk about it, but that I had no idea he was with Jayde the whole time. By the time I finish, my hands are shaking uncontrollably.

Jake's eyes are wide as I finish, and he shakes his head as he lets out a long breath.

"That's crazy. There's no way Jase would cheat on you, A. No way."

He shakes his head again to accentuate his point. I find myself shaking my head in agreement, but I'm starting to doubt how sure I am of that after hearing they spent all day together.

Jake looks at me pointedly as if he can read my mind.

"Come on, A. This is Jase we're talking about. He's one of the few good ones left."

I look into Jake's eyes.

"I know he is, but I've been pushing him away so much lately that maybe he's had enough. It's all so messed up. I don't know how to talk to him about how I've been feeling. Some days I feel like we're miles apart and I don't know how to close the distance anymore. Other days we are so in sync that I can't imagine how I ever feel far away from him at all. I've been so selfish since Tate died."

I bury my face in my hands because I can't bear to look Jake in the eyes.

"I've been selfish with everyone, Jake. You included. I am barely keeping myself together lately. I don't have room for anything else, which sounds terrible as I say it out loud, but it's true."

"I don't think you know how to be selfish, A," Jake interrupts me and reaches out for my hand.

"I'm not the same person anymore, Jake."

"With good reason. You couldn't possibly be. I'm not the same either."

Jake looks at me and for a moment I think I may cry. I swallow loudly.

"I thought I was okay last summer, but I think I was just avoiding all of it. After the plea bargain and knowing that three of them are getting away with it, I lost it. I lost the ability to keep everything shoved down inside of me. It came up and over the sides of me like a volcano. I don't know how to explain it better than that. I'm angry and hurt and scared and so incredibly sad all at once. I don't know if I want to cry, scream or break something most of the time. I don't know how to be happy anymore. I don't how to make things go back to how they used to be. It's not the same."

Jake gets up and picks some of the sunflowers, handing them to me as he does.

"A, things will never be the same. You can't expect them to be and neither can Jase."

I gather the sunflowers into a bunch and sit them on my lap.

"But I think that's what Jase wants. I want that, too … for him and I at least."

"What is it that bothers you so much, A? What are you afraid of telling Jase? Do you want to break up with him?"

My head snaps up and I shake my head.

"No, of course I don't, but that's the point. I don't think that I'm good for him. I want to be selfish and keep him to myself, but I'm not sure that I am what he needs anymore, even if I am what he wants. It doesn't matter what I want. I know that Jase wants to be with me. I know he loves me, but I'm not what's best for him. He's ready to settle with only being okay with me instead of being really happy again with someone else. I don't like that he's willing to give up or settle for things because of me. I can't handle that. He deserves more than that."

Jake sits back down on the swing gently.

"A, if Jase wants to be with you because he loves you, that's his choice. If he chooses to stay behind and pass on the fellowship, again, that's his choice. You can't decide what is best for him. That's not fair. He gets a say in this, right?"

I look at Jake sadly and shake my head.

"What if he chooses wrong? What if I let him go down the wrong path simply because I am too afraid to let him go? He'll do that. You know he will. He'll cling to me if he thinks I need him. He'll never go."

The realization of this hits me like a ton of bricks. I feel like I can't breathe.

"A, if you're so sure that being with you is wrong for Jase, then why is it bothering you so much that he spent time with someone else? If you keep pushing him away because you think that's what is better for him, isn't he's only doing what you want him to do?"

I let that sink in for a moment. Jake is right. I can't push Jase away over and over and then get upset and frustrated when I push him into the arms of someone else. I look up at Jake as he stares at me intently.

"I don't know if being together is the right thing anymore."

As soon as I say it out loud, my hand moves quickly to my mouth to cover it. I didn't realize that was what I was going to say. I hadn't planned on it and yet, it came out anyway. Jake shakes his head at me again.

"The right thing for who — you or him?"

"Jase will always be the best thing — the right thing — for me. Even when I'm angry and frustrated, he always sees the best in me. He sees me the way I wish everyone would, the way I wish I could see myself. But if I hold him back from his dreams, then I'm not good for him anymore. I can't do that. I won't do that."

Jake looks as surprised as I feel.

"Are you really going to break up with Jase, A? I thought you two would be together forever."

I look down at my hands and absent-mindedly pull at the petals of the sunflowers.

"I don't want to, but I think that he should want more than what I'm giving him right now. I think Jase of all people deserves more. He's given me so much. I don't know what to do anymore, Jake. Part of me wants to let him go because I know it's better for him. I feel like an anchor holding him back from moving forward, but a larger part of me wants him to tell me that I'm crazy and that he would never leave and I'm the only one for him. And that makes me incredibly selfish."

"You are different, A," Jake says to me softly as he reaches out for my hand again. "But I don't think you are selfish. I'm not sure I agree with what you're saying, but I understand it. I still think you should talk to Jase about all of this, though. You keep forgetting about his feelings in all of this."

I start pulling the seeds out of the middle of the sunflower. There are only a few that the birds left behind.

"If I say these things to Jase, he'll insist that he wants to be with me no matter what because he thinks it's the right thing to do. Even though that's what I want to hear, I don't know if it's good for him to devote so much of his life to me when we're so young. He should be having the time of his life right now. He has this chance of a lifetime opportunity that he worked so hard for, and instead of being excited and celebrating, we had a fight about him not wanting to leave without me. He needs to be able to do it without me and I don't think he'll leave me behind."

"A, maybe you are unintentionally holding him back in some ways, but you can't change what happened to you and what we all have to live with now. Maybe you need to heal a little on your own so that you don't feel like you rely on him so much. But I will say, knowing Jase the way I do, he won't let you go without a fight. You need to be honest with him and tell him everything you just told me."

"I don't know what I'm more scared of — him agreeing with me or him fighting me on it. I'm not sure my heart can take either to be honest. I'm so scared of losing him, but I know what he'll give up chasing me down the rabbit hole that I'm lost in. That is the exact reason why I can't tell him the truth."

Jake sighs next to me.

"I don't understand. If you can't tell him the truth, what are you going to do?"

I open my palm and let the sunflower seeds and bright yellow petals fall to the ground. The wind picks up and blows the petals across the lawn before it carries them out of view completely.

"I'm going to lie to him, Jake. I'm going to lie through my teeth. It's the only way."

# 30 - Jase

Music fills the air around me making it hard to hear. I am trying to have a good time at the party, but all I can think about is A.

*Nothing new.*

Jesse hasn't seen her since they got back from the cemetery earlier today and she still hasn't answered one call or text from me. I thought for sure she'd end up coming home for Ryan's party, but I haven't seen her yet. I keep scanning the crowd for her face, but I'm disappointed every time my eyes wander through the faces and I don't find hers.

As I turn to scan the crowd once more, I see Jayde and Ashleigh dancing. My stomach jumps as Jayde locks eyes with me and smiles. I turn my head quickly pretending not to notice her and make a beeline for the summerhouse. I close the sliding glass door behind me, and the music and noise of the crowd dies down a bit.

I open the fridge and reach down for a beer when I hear a familiar voice behind me.

"Hey."

I spin around quickly and find A standing in front of me. My heart starts pounding immediately. I don't say a word and don't give her time to say anything else. I gather her up in my arms and hold her tight to me. I pull her close to me and she curls into me like she always does. We stay this way for a few long moments, but when she pulls away from me gently, it doesn't feel like long enough.

She peers up at me with wide eyes and there are tears forming in the corners that she won't allow to spill over to her cheeks. I lightly kiss the corner of each eye and feel the saltiness of her tears on my lips.

"I'm so sorry, A."

I reach out for her and touch the side of her face. She puts her hand over mine and stares back at me. She pulls my hand away from her face and pulls me out the front door and onto the porch.

She leans against the wood railing and turns to face me. She smiles slowly and pulls me close to her once more. She leans her head on my chest and I kiss the top of her head.

"Nothing happened, A. I swear to you. Nothing happened at all. I had a few drinks with Chris, and he introduced me to Jayde. She flirted with me at the bar and at Chris' place and I didn't do anything to stop it. I'm sorry for that, but I swear on everything important to the both of us that is as far as it went. Jayde and Chris spent the night together in his room while I slept on the couch. That's the whole story."

She wraps both arms around me and squeezes.

"I'm sorry, Jase," she whispers softly. "I got jealous and overreacted, but … "

She pauses and pulls away from me. She takes a few steps off the front porch and shakes her head, staring at her feet.

"But what, A?"

I step down from the porch and follow her onto the front lawn. She shakes her head again, but keeps her eyes trained on her feet. I grab for her hand, but she pulls it away from me. When she looks up at me her cheeks are shiny with tears.

"I don't think I can do this anymore."

Her voice is so low that I almost don't hear her over the bass of the music out back.

"Don't think you can do what?"

I hear the tremble in my voice, but I don't care.

"Too much has changed, Jase. I'm different and you're different and maybe it's for the best if we take some time to ourselves to figure out what we want."

She looks away from me again, but I watch the tears continue to slide down her cheeks. They form wet spots on both sides of her collarbone. It takes me a minute to find my voice again.

"You're breaking up with me? A, I told you nothing happened!"

I hear the panic in my voice — the desperation.

*She can't do this.*

"A, please. Don't do this."

She finally looks at me, but something has changed in her eyes. Instead of pain, there's a determination there now.

"This isn't only about Jayde. There are reasons why you flirted with her last night. There are reasons why you didn't call me last night and why we spent the night apart. It's probably the same reasons that you spent the day with her today. Things have changed between us and we shouldn't stay together because we feel obligated to. You should be able to date other people if that's what you want to do. I don't want to be an anchor for you, Jase, and I feel like I've already become one."

My world spins out of control.

*This can't be real.*

"A, this is crazy. Things haven't changed between us. Yes, we fight sometimes, but that's how relationships work. I don't want to date anyone else. I love you. I only want to be with you. I'm frustrated a lot lately, yes, but I don't want to break up. I want to spend my life with you. I can't picture my life without you in it."

I close the gap between us and kiss her without hesitation. She relaxes beneath my touch and for a moment, the hard look in her eyes disappears. Her eyes flutter closed, and the kiss continues. When we finally pull apart, I'm breathing heavy. I watch her chest rise and fall quickly, too.

"Please," I beg her. "Please, don't do this."

*Please, don't do this to me.*

She bites her lip nervously and won't meet my eyes.

"It's for the best, Jase."

"The best for who?! You love me. I know you do. Why are you doing this?"

I watch a confusing surge of emotions flash through her face. She looks into my eyes.

"I love you, Jase. I will always love you, even if you can't love me after this, but I am not in love with you."

She stands tall and strong as my world bottoms out from under me. The past few months flash by in memory and I wonder how long she's felt this way. I think about the kiss we had just moments ago and refuse to believe her.

"You're lying. I don't understand why, but you are. You don't kiss someone the way you kiss me when you don't love them. I don't know why you're pushing me away, A, but I'm begging you not to do this. I know you think I'm the strong one always taking care of you, but I can't make it without you. Don't you get that?"

Her lip trembles and something breaks behind her hard stare. She takes a step toward me, reaching for my hand. She looks up at me, tears streaming down her face. Her other hand gently touches my chin, and I can see in her eyes that she's in pain.

"A, please," I beg her. "Talk to me. Whatever is going on, we'll figure it out, together —like we always do. Please."

Before she can answer, the entire group of our friends walks around the side of the house. Ryan and Ashleigh are arm in arm. Ace and Jesse are shoving each other jokingly. Zac, Austin, Mikey, Alex, and Jackson have drinks in hand and are talking animatedly to each other.

"There they are!" Ryan says to the group. "We've been looking for you two everywhere."

"I didn't know you were back, A. Where'd ya go earlier?" Jesse says as he pushes Ace once more.

A won't break her gaze from mine. The color has drained from her face and she looks like a deer caught in headlights. I blink a few times but can't think of anything to say at all.

Zac catches the look on my face and stops in his tracks. This causes a few of the guys to bump into each other. Ryan looks from my face to Ayla's face and then back again. I keep staring into Ayla's eyes, but the vulnerability that was there moments ago has disappeared. She drops her hands to her side and avoids my gaze, pulling away from me.

"Uh, you guys are in the middle of something, aren't ya?" Zac says quietly.

Ayla simply looks down at her feet and shakes her head slowly, which for some reason makes me angry. The sheer casualness of all of this makes me feel like I'm dreaming it.

"I said what I needed to say," she says softly.

"So, we're done here? That's it?!"

My voice rises with anger and hurt and a million other things that I can't make sense of. I turn to look at the guys again.

"She wants to break up. That basically sums it up, right?"

My voice is angry and carries farther than I mean it to. I watch as other people at the party pick up their heads and notice us now, too.

"Jase—" A starts to say, taking a step toward me.

I put my hands up to stop her.

"You said what you needed to say. You aren't in love with me. Fine. Great. Let's make it official. We're done."

Without so much as a glance back at the rest of my friends, I shove my hands in my pockets and stalk to my truck. I put it in drive before I've even fully gotten inside and spin the tires the entire way out of the driveway, making a scene and not caring one bit.

I glance in the rearview mirror before I pull out onto the road and catch a glimpse of the guys standing where I left them, mouths open in shock, but as usual, A has disappeared.

# 31 - Ayla

Nobody ever wants to talk about grief — real grief. The kind of grief that makes you obsessive, compulsive and angry all the time, pushing away anyone who wants to help you. The kind of grief that fills up all other parts of your life leaving them a shade of grey. The kind of grief that changes who a person is on the inside, twisting pieces of themselves to the point of breaking. Grief doesn't let up with time. If anything, it gets stronger with each day that passes — a torturously powerful shot straight to the heart.

Loss does horrible things to your mind and body, and most people who've never experienced it themselves won't understand it by description alone.

Losing Tate is a loss I wasn't prepared to experience. It took me by surprise and the hail of emotions that followed continue to confuse and amaze me even now.

We all lost Tate that night. Mr. Gematti's grief was and is raw and powerful. He is loud about it and cries unabashedly, something I had never seen prior to that night. I wouldn't have guessed the man knew how to cry. Ryan's grief is full of guilt and regret. His tears fall for the loss of the brother he knew and loved, and for the part of his brother's life he never knew until his death. Jesse grieves for the friend he lost by drowning his emotions and avoiding feeling anything at all. He doesn't understand what he feels, so he drinks. He feels guilty about pulling away from Tate the past few years, so he drinks. He doesn't know how to help the Gematti family, so he drinks. We all grieve in our own way for Tate. We all share that same bond that binds us tighter than ever before. Even though some of us are spinning out of control at times, that bond tethers us back to one another. None of us get to see Tate or talk to him or hear his laugh. It's a universal loss across the board.

Losing someone you love who's still alive is an entirely different kind of loss. It opens you up and splits you apart. It hollows you out and makes you feel empty. Telling Jase I'm not in love him was the hardest thing I've ever had to do in my life. I've told many white lies to the people I love to protect them. I've hid my own feelings so as not to hurt others, but I've never had to say something to someone I love knowing it will hurt them. Telling Jase that it is over between us because I'm not in love with him anymore was a lie — a difficult one for me to make sound convincing. I almost crumbled and took it all back.

Walking away from him knowing he was no longer mine was devastating. I walked around the side of the summerhouse and collapsed. My body shook with tears and my heart was beating so hard that it felt like it would burst. I couldn't catch my breath and the world spun around me. I don't know how long I laid there — my cheek plastered to the grass and sand with my tears — until I caught my breath again. It felt like years. I managed to crawl into the house and up into my shower before anyone else even noticed.

Now I'm a zombie. Days end and then morning comes, and I start the cycle all over again, but I don't engage in the middle part. Life is happening around me, but all I can focus on and think about is Jase. I go through the motions each day, but everything feels different now. Home no longer feels like home. Everything feels less. Everything is less.

The hardest part is the not knowing. Not knowing how Jase is doing or what he is doing. Not knowing if he hates me or if we'll ever be able to be friends again. Not knowing who he's talking to, if Jayde is attached to him now or if he's met someone new. Not knowing if he's having as hard a time with this as I am. I hate the not knowing. It makes me crazy. I no longer feel crazy — I think I am.

And now I want to talk to him so badly. I want to run to him and tell him all the things that he wanted me to come to him and talk about before. I want to spill every thought in my head and let the words tumble out and pour over him. I want him to know how much I love him and how grateful I am for him. I want to talk to him and hear his voice. I miss his touch and his smell and the way he squints his eyes when he smiles. Even though I know this is the best thing for him, I want to undo it all so that I can have him back. But I won't, so I simply suffer in silence.

I cry all the time now and everywhere. I cry when I'm in the shower. I cry while driving. I cry in bed while I lie awake all night staring at the clock through my tears. I'm hollow with an endless supply of tears.

It comes in waves. There are hours that seem better than others and I get through them somehow. Then a new wave hits me at the most random time and knocks me over. I've never felt an ache like this. It's all consuming. It's going to strangle me if I let it.

*Part of me wants to just let it.*

# 32 - Jase

I don't know how to do this. I don't know how to be me without A. I can't stand the idea of living without her with me. I don't know what happened or why she is doing this. I feel empty and angry and confused, but mostly I'm heart broken.

I feel as though I've lost a limb. I keep reaching out for it, feeling if it's still there. Then the realization that it's really gone hits once again and life seems to stop.

It feels that way, but life doesn't actually stop. Morning turns into night which turns into morning again and the days pass. People move around me and talk around me, but I feel like I'm an outsider. I don't know how to engage in the mundane of everyday life any longer because my life is no longer meaningful. I'm suffering in such a way that returning to regular things seems trivial. I get frustrated that everyone else around me has gone back to normal life. I don't think anyone else understands what this is like.

I spend most of my time working on projects for my clients. It's the only time my mind isn't focused solely on A. When I'm working on a piece of furniture, everything else falls away. Nothing else seems to do that for me anymore, not even working on the renovation house. There are too many memories of us woven through that house. I haven't slept there the past few weeks. I sleep in my childhood bedroom at dad's house — a place where memories of A don't fill every space.

I'm not sure how we got here. I don't even know when we turned off the road we were on to end up where we are. I keep thinking about her looking me in the eye and telling me she isn't in love with me. It's like hearing it for the first time every time. That was the last thing I expected to come out of her mouth.

*I will always love you, but I'm not in love with you.*

My heart clenches. I cringe outwardly as I relive hearing it. One sentence that changed it all. One sentence that makes me question everything.

My phone vibrates and I look down hoping to see A's name on the screen. My heart drops when I see it's a text from Jayde. I shake my head feeling stupid. I wonder how long I'll continue to hope that she'll call or text telling me it's all been a mistake. It feels like I haven't spoken to her in months even though it's only been a few weeks. So much has changed in such a short amount of time that it feels like much longer.

I clench my jaw and swipe the phone to read the text.

*U free 2nite? I want to c u.*

I shake my head once more as I scroll through all of the unanswered texts from her going back to the day I dropped her off at Ashleigh's. The same day that Ayla broke up with me. Jayde sent me a message almost as soon as I left the driveway that night. I ignored it and I've ignored every one since. The girl doesn't give up.

I toss my phone on the table next to me and go back to the coffee table sitting in front of me. I've been sanding for hours but can't seem to get it just right. I try to quiet my mind. My hands run over the surface without thinking about it. I let my eyes follow the grain in the wood, but I can't seem to focus.

I hear a cough behind me and find dad standing in the doorway.

"Time for a break," he says to me as more of an order than a question.

He nods his head out the back window toward the deck and I follow him through the house until he reaches his destination. He sits in the old rocker his father made with him and motions for me to sit in the matching one a few feet away. On the small table between us are two glasses and an open bottle. Each glass is already filled with two fingers of whiskey. My father doesn't drink much or often, but this is somewhat of a father-son tradition. It's something that his father did with him, and now he does with me, and it usually means he wants to have a serious heart to heart.

He hands one of the glasses to me and takes the other for himself before sitting back and resting his head on the high back of the chair. I swallow what's in the glass and sit back myself, resting my head in the same manner.

"How you doing, kid?" dad asks me as he sips his whiskey.

"I've been better, Pops. I miss her," my voice catches a bit, so I pause for a moment and clear my throat. "I miss her so much."

Dad only nods and stays quiet for a moment. He pours more whiskey into my glass when he sees that mine is empty.

"It's not an easy thing to do — letting someone go who you love. I know you love her, Jase. Sometimes, as you get older you grow apart and things change.

That's what happened with your mother and me. Letting your mom leave was one of the hardest things I had to do, but it's what she needed to be happy. She wasn't happy with me anymore and I think that's why she spent so much time and energy trying to escape by drinking because she felt trapped. We were young parents, and she wasn't ready for it. You're the best thing that ever happened to us — both of us — but she felt like getting married so young made her miss out on things. I don't think it's the same story for you and Ayla. It may not seem that way now, but I don't think this is the end for you two. You may have to let her go for a while so she can figure out how to come back to you herself — on her own terms."

I dump the remaining whiskey into my mouth and it burns down my throat. The ache in my chest that never seems to go away magnifies with the burn. I nod at dad knowing I'm not ready to lose her forever. It gives me hope knowing someone else believes in us the way that I do, but the mere mention of her name brings her face to mind immediately and I'm struck with an overwhelming sense of loss. What I wouldn't do to see her right now — to reach out and touch her face, to reach for her hand, to kiss her once more. The raw emotion that I try to keep buried most days threatens to take over and I place the empty glass on the table next to me.

I get up from the chair and dad stands up at the same time. He reaches for me and hugs me tight.

"Love you, Pops," I say, my voice thick with tears I am not ready to shed.

"Love you, kid."

I gather myself together and head into the house for a shower. I turn on the hot water and let it run over me, burning everywhere the water touches. I grab for the handle to make the water even hotter and let the stinging sensation take away all the thoughts in my head. For the briefest of moments, I get lost in the physical pain so much so that the ache in my chest subsides.

# 33 - Ayla

I'm packing my bags once again to head home and it's hard to believe yet another summer has ended. The past few weeks have gone by too fast and too slow all at once. I haven't seen or spoken to Jase in weeks, but it feels like years. Not having him to ground me, to come home to, to talk to — it all makes me miss home in New York so much more than I ever have before.

Ryan calls for me from downstairs and I can hear the clatter of dishes in the kitchen. Zac decided that we'd have a big dinner at the summerhouse for our last night together and they've been in the kitchen cooking while I pack my things. I don't know if they invited Jase. I have been too embarrassed to ask. I don't know if Jase will show up if they did. I try not to get my hopes up, but the thought of leaving for New York without seeing Jase at least one more time makes tears appear in my eyes. I have no idea what I would say to him if he did or if he would even speak to me, but somehow seeing him would be enough.

When I walk into the kitchen, I can't help but grin. Jesse, Ryan and Zac are all wearing aprons and cooking. Ace, Austin and Mikey are setting the table while Alex and Jackson are out back cooking on the grill.

I put on an apron and help Jesse cut vegetables for a salad that I won't eat. He catches my eye and grins at me. I smile back, but my mind is on Jase the entire time.

When it's time to sit down to eat, I realize the table is set for ten, but Jase's seat remains empty as the guys pile plates high with lobster, clams, macaroni and cheese and corn on the cob. The salad that Jesse and I worked on remains mostly untouched.

Ryan catches me eyeing the empty seat and reaches for my hand under the table to squeeze it. I squeeze back as a memory of my first night meeting Tate floods my mind. I reach out with my other hand for the glass of water in front of me and furiously try to swallow any emotions that battle back. The one good thing that has come from all of this is that I don't feel like drinking alcohol as much anymore. For the first time in a long time, I want to feel this pain instead of numbing it. I need to feel it to make it real because it still feels like a dream weeks later.

We finish dinner and the guys refuse to let me clean up. Alex hustles me outside to help him build a fire in between the house and the bungalows. I setup chairs while Alex piles the wood in our pit. When he gets it going, I sit directly in the sand in front of the fire. Jesse appears with his guitar and begins to play. I watch as the flames dance to his music. The rest of the guys trickle out of the back door and gather around the fire. Ryan has invited some other friends of ours and they begin to appear shortly after.

Music and laughter fill the air, but I feel like I'm floating above it all. I feel removed from everything that's happening around me as I'm lost in my own thoughts. I stand up, brush off the sand from my legs and feet, and walk toward the house. I hear a burst of laughter and turn towards the sound while I continue to walk. With my head turned behind me, I walk right into someone else.

"I'm so sorry," I begin before I fully turn around and that's when I realize it's Jase.

All of the breath rushes out of me. No thought runs through my mind. I'm completely blank. I don't know what to say or do, so my feet stay locked into place and I stand there dumbfounded. I realize my mouth is hanging slightly open, so I close it and try a small smile.

Jase returns the smile and reaches his hand out for mine. His touch brings electrifying currents up and down the surface of my skin and it instantly wakes me up. My eyes lock with his as his thumb grazes the tops of my fingers.

"I know you're surprised to see me," Jase says after he clears his throat. "I wasn't sure whether I should come or not, but I couldn't let you go back North without talking to you first and saying goodbye."

I'm afraid the tears I've been fighting all night may finally win, so I only nod and squeeze his hand that's still holding mine. I walk slowly to the front of the house with Jase trailing behind me, our hands still linked.

The noise of the fire and music and laughter dies down as we walk around the front. I sit on the first step and Jase sits next to me.

"Hi," I say quietly, awkwardly smiling up at him.

Jase laughs quickly and then catches himself.

"Hi."

I start to tell him how much I miss him, how I'm so happy that he came and that I was hoping he would, but before I can say a word, he stops me.

"You don't need to say anything. I wanted to see you before you left. I wanted to hold your hand and see you smile one more time. And I wanted to say goodbye to you. A proper goodbye because I didn't handle it well the last time we spoke."

Jase lets go of my hand before he continues and even though I want to reach for it the second he lets go, something about the look on his face stops me.

"I understand we have to go different directions right now. I know that the fellowship is my dream, and you have to find yours. I hate the thought of us not being together, but I know that it's what we both need to do right now."

My heart sinks and the world stops.

"You do?"

My voice is almost a whisper.

Hearing him confirm everything I've been worried about shatters whatever pieces of my heart are still left.

"I know you're trying to work through a lot of things, and I need to let you go to do that. I will always love you, Ayla, but I know that I'm not what you need at the moment. Just know that if you ever do need me, I will always be here for you. Always."

My hands are shaking so I hide them underneath me. I shake my head at Jase but can't seem to find my voice. He stands up slowly and places both hands on either side of my face. I silently plead with him to kiss my lips, but he places a soft kiss on the top of my head instead. When my eyes flutter back open, he is standing over me.

"Goodbye, A."

Jase turns and walks away from me.

"Jase, wait–"

I hop up from the step and jog to catch up with him. He turns to face me again and I wrap myself around him tightly. At first, he doesn't move and then his arms encircle me. The scent of his soap fills the air and I try to memorize it. After a few moments like this, I pull back and look up at him.

A million things run through my mind. I want to tell him it was all a lie. I want to beg him to spend the last night in my bed with me. I want to never let go of him, but I do. I let my arms fall to my sides instead.

"Goodbye, Jase."

He smiles at me and turns around again. I run into the house and up into my room before I let a single tear fall. When the bedroom door closes behind me, I let it all out. Every emotion that I've been experiencing the past few weeks comes charging out of me at once. I bury my face in my pillow and cry. Stifled sobs echo into my empty room.

I cry so hard and so loudly that I don't hear my bedroom door open and close softly. Jesse sits down next to me on my bed, pulls me into his arms and holds me while I cry every last tear I have stored. He doesn't say a word, but simply places his hand on the back of my head and lets me cry.

We sit like this for a long time. When the sobs finally slow down, I take a deep breath and pick my head up from Jesse's shoulder. He reaches up slowly and dries my tears. The intimacy of the moment embarrasses me, so I put my arms around him again. I return my head to his shoulder, so I don't have to look into his eyes.

"Thank you," I whisper into his ear and he nods in return.

I wish it were that easy to take someone's pain away. I wish Jesse could wipe away all of it the way he did my tears. Instead, the tears I cried release a thick feeling of despair in the room. I can feel it weighing us down in silence as I wallow in it.

"I was ruining it all. I don't want to, but I have to let him go." I whisper, my voice disappearing into silence at the end.

Jesse holds me tighter.

"I know, A."

It's the only thing that he says, but I know in the way that he holds me that he does.

# 34 - Jase

"Thank you, sir. I'm honored and so very grateful for this opportunity. I'm looking forward to working with you this summer."

I hang up the phone and place it on my desk. I just spoke with my mentor assigned to me for the fellowship. He asked me questions about my work and even told me the program was impressed by my eye for design.

*Someone from Sam Maloof Woodworkers, Inc. told me they were impressed by me.*

It's crazy to think about, and yet, while I should be floating on air right now full of excitement and pride, I'm not. I feel like a deflated balloon. I bob up and down, but I never quite make it off the floor.

I stare at Ayla's picture in front of me. It's a black and white photo of her laughing. Her head is back, her eyes are bright, and she looks like she doesn't have a care in the world. Jesse took the photo at a barbecue years ago and it's been on my desk ever since.

*And there it is again.*

That constant feeling that the world isn't right without her here with me. It fades in and out, but never quite seems to go away. It's been almost three months since she's been back in New York, but the feeling seems to get stronger and more persistent as time passes.

I keep thinking about what I should be doing with her or what we should be planning. I'm caught up in this cycle of regret and loss. I can't decide if I'm hurt or angry. Most of the time it's both. What I do know for sure is that I love Ayla more than I realized. I love her with every fiber of my being. She's the one person who could make me happy and furious all in the same day, but I love that we always seem to find our way back to each other. And that's what I keep telling myself. That's how I get through the really difficult moments that turn into difficult days.

I keep telling myself that we'll find our way back to one another. It's this middle part that I'm having a hard time with.

This week is especially challenging. Under normal circumstances, Ayla would be staying with me for the week. She has spent the last two Thanksgivings with dad and me, but she won't be joining us this year. The week looms ahead of me empty and taunting. It's usually my favorite holiday, but this year I don't want to celebrate. If dad didn't love it so much, I'd ask him if we could skip it altogether. It feels pointless without A here with me. Everything feels pointless and empty now.

I don't know what to do with myself anymore. I never realized how much time I spent with A or talking to her. The days stretch out infinitely long and trying to get through each one is exhausting. I don't know how much more I can take.

I glance down at my phone and fight the never-ending urge to call her. I pick it up, cycle through my recent calls and texts, and even though I already know it'll happen, my heart squeezes when I don't see her name there. It feels like I lose her more with each day that passes. Every night I think about how much farther away she is compared to the day before. It's like watching a slow-moving ship sail away in the distance. You can barely make out the silhouette anymore and your feet are stuck on shore. You can't bring it back. You can't call out. You have to stand there and watch it move farther and farther away from you. It's the last thing you want to do, but you have no choice. The worst part — the thought that tortures me every moment of every day — is knowing that if and when she is ever ready to look back in my direction, she may be so far away that she can no longer see me.

I have no control. I want her to come back to me more than anything I've ever wanted in my life, but I don't want to pull her back to me. I want her to come back because she's realized, just like I have, that life is not complete when we aren't together.

We are two halves of a greater whole. We were before we ever met. Our souls are intertwined. They never had a choice in the matter, like a plant twisting toward the sun.

I jump as the phone buzzes in my hand. It's a text message from Chris.

*Drinks tonight? Meet me at the bar?*

I shake my head, knowing Jayde probably convinced him to send it. I quickly type a response.

*Will Jayde be there?*

The phone buzzes immediately.

*Most likely.*

I sigh and shake my head. I look around the room knowing I have nothing better to do. I'm not sure I want to go, but it beats sitting here torturing myself. I write back to Chris.

*Sure. C u later.*

# 35 – Ayla

The world is spinning wildly around me and I can't seem to make it slow down. I feel like I missed something along the way. Somehow, I've been left behind and now I am lost.

All along I thought that Jase would have a hard time letting me go. I know it's what is best for him, but the separation of us was like carving myself in half. I haven't been the same since. I don't think I ever could be the same again. It broke my heart to let him go but watching him release me so easily was another level of pain — one I wasn't prepared for.

The past few months have been hard to tackle alone. When I lost Tate — when we all lost Tate — we were experiencing it together. I had support and understanding from my closest friends because we were all going through the same thing. This battle I lost alone. The aftermath I am still battling alone. No one else understands what this is like because as far as everyone else is concerned, it was my choice. And the reality of this stings like hot coals searing through my heart.

*This was my choice.*

Knowing it doesn't make it easier. Somehow it makes it worse. Realizing that I was right all along is a kind of pain I can't describe. Sometimes I convince myself of things because I want other people to prove me wrong. The idea that Jase is better off without me has been floating through my mind and heart for a while, but having it confirmed is a new kind of torture I wasn't fully ready to experience.

The week of Thanksgiving was the worst. Seeing the pictures on social media of him out with friends drinking and having a good time while my world was bottoming out from under me made it all hurt worse. It made the pain real — sharp and deep.

The holidays are hard enough when you feel alone. Everyone else is cheerful and wants to spend time together laughing and happy and all I want to do is stay in bed with the covers over my head. My family doesn't understand. They try to, but after the first few weeks I think they got tired of me sulking. I can't seem to snap out of this. Part of the reason is I don't want to. I don't know how to make anyone else understand that letting him go means accepting that it's over.

I feel lost right now, so instead of moving forward or moving on, I stand as still as possible. Everything and everyone else continues to move around me and I begin to wonder if this is how it's always been — me standing still while life spins around me.

I look down at the necklace my mother gave me as an early Christmas gift. I touch the charm on the necklace, fingers feeling for the roughly etched words, "Fear Not Change." I look at the outline of the butterfly underneath it and know it's time to let go. Even though it's the last thing I want to do right now, it feels necessary.

I imagine all of it — the pain, the heartache, the tears, the terrifying unknown set before me without him — as a butterfly that I'm setting free. Somehow, it's easier for me to let it go that way.

# 36 - Jase

It's New Year's Eve and Ryan is throwing one of his parties tonight. Jayde has been texting me on and off since Thanksgiving, but I still don't respond. I've become good friends with Chris, and while it's pretty obvious that he really likes Jayde, she goes out of her way to flirt with me in front of him. It feels wrong, even now. Every time she sends me a text or smiles at me or touches my arm, A is always at the back of my mind. Maybe it will always be that way. I'm not sure if that will ever change.

*How long should I wait for A? How long do I believe in something everyone else thinks is over?*

I pick up my phone and suck in a breath of air. There's a new text message on my screen, but it's not from Jayde like I assumed. Ayla's name flashes across my screen and my heart leaps. I quickly open the message as my heart thuds rapidly in my chest.

*Hey, I know it's been weird for us, but I wanted you to know that I'm thinking of you. Hope you enjoyed the holidays and wanted to wish you an early Happy New Year!*

The message is followed by three hearts and nothing else. I start to type a message back, but realize I have no idea what to say. There are so many things I want to send, but everything I begin to type doesn't sound right so I delete it as quickly as I begin to type it.

She's always had this power over me — this ability to pull me toward her even when I feel farther away from her than I ever have. I don't know what makes me do it, but I delete the message from my phone so that I don't have to stare at it any longer. I feel guilty as soon as I do, but there's also a sense of relief. The pressure to respond is gone now that it's not sitting unanswered on my phone.

# 37 - Ayla

"Happy New Year!"

The voices echo one another on my phone, and I laugh out loud despite having a miserable night. My phone rang the second the clock struck midnight and I wasn't surprised to see Ryan's number. I can tell the guys are on speakerphone because they are all talking over one another and I can hear people singing along with music in the background.

"We love you."

"You should be here celebrating with us, A."

"What are you doing tonight?"

"Why aren't you here with us?"

I smile to myself.

"I love you guys, too! I didn't go out tonight. I'm home alone, actually. My sisters are both out and my parents are with some friends."

*I've been sitting alone feeling sorry for myself all night because Jase didn't text me back.*

That's the truth, but I don't say it out loud. Both sisters had invited me out with them, as did my parents and a few other friends, but I said no to them all.

I hear Ashleigh's voice in the background and her and Ryan laughing. The background noise dies down and I realize someone has taken me off of speakerphone.

"Why are you alone, A?"

I hear the concern in Jesse's voice, and I'm surprised that he also sounds sober.

"Jesse! Happy New Year!"

I try to avoid the question, but he sees right through it.

"You should be here with us and you know it. I miss you, A."

I nod into the phone as if Jesse can see me. My voice catches as I try to respond.

"I know, Jesse. I miss you, too. I didn't want to make anyone uncomfortable there and I didn't feel like going out here, so I stayed home. I feel kind of lost, Jess — I don't know what to do with myself anymore."

"You belong here, more than anyone else does. Everyone is here tonight. Even your best friend Jayde … "

I think he meant it as a joke, but Jesse's voice trails off as he realizes that may not be what I wanted to hear. My heart drops. Even though I had suspected Jayde would be there with Ashleigh tonight, it doesn't stop the jealousy from raging within me at the sound of her name.

"I'm sorry. I didn't mean… you should be here. That's all. I hate that you aren't. We could have hung out together. Me and you — screw everyone else."

I smile and try to find my voice.

"It's okay, Jess. It's just— "

What's the word I'm looking for? Hard? Weird? Uncomfortable? Heart-wrenching?

"It's just different now."

"I know it is, A. You and Jase are different now. But you and everyone else are the same. You can't avoid seeing him forever because that means you're avoiding all of us, too."

Again, having it confirmed by someone else that Jase and I are no longer the same hurts deeper than when I think it myself.

"I'm not avoiding you or anyone else, Jesse. I promise. I'll see you in March for Spring Break. It's only a couple of months away."

There's a long pause where neither of us say anything and I feel like I hurt Jesse's feelings even though I had no intention of doing that.

"Don't be so sad, A. I think Jase seems happy. You should be, too. I want you to be."

"I want to be, too. I will be. I think I need help, Jess. I don't want to feel this way anymore."

There's a long pause before Jesse responds.

"A — maybe it's worth talking to your parents or maybe going to see someone … you know professionally or whatever."

I'm surprised by Jesse's suggestion even though I've been considering seeing a therapist myself. He continues before I can respond.

"Ace suggested I talk to someone about my drinking, which at first pissed me off and made me drink more, but I had a really bad night about a month ago, so I finally agreed. I think it's been helping, A. Maybe it can help you, too."

I nod into the receiver and realize Jesse can't see me.

"Maybe it will, Jesse. I'll think about it. I promise."

We say our goodbyes, but Jesse's words linger in my head long after we've hung up. I touch my hand to my cheek and am surprised when I feel the tears. I had been crying the entire time and didn't even notice. My tears have a mind of their own lately.

I think about Jase being at the same party as Jayde tonight. My mind begins to play out events that my inner jealous demon dreams up. I imagine them laughing and sharing a kiss at midnight the way we always have. My chest feels tight. I keep telling myself that I want him to be happy, even if that means he is with someone else. I keep telling myself that I did this because I want him to have something more than me. I keep telling myself that this is how things should be. I think if I repeat it in my head enough times, I'll actually start to believe it. I want all of those things to be true. I want to be a selfless person who cares more about his happiness than my own, but the truth is, I hate this with everything in me. I want to be his and I want him to be mine. I don't like the idea of someone else making him happy or making him laugh. I don't want to think about him touching her, her kissing him, or him wanting her or anyone else for that matter. I want to be the one he shares his life with, but the damage is done. I made my choice.

I was trying to give him a gift, but I didn't think about trying to simply give him what he's always wanted instead … me. He only wanted all of me and I was too stubborn to give it to him. I was too scared to open myself up to him the way that I used to.

I thought I was broken, but I wanted him to prove to me that I wasn't. I wanted him to prove to me that I was enough. Instead of telling him that, I pushed him away and pretended it was for his own good. Now, it's too late to take it all back. I look down at my hands in my lap, puddled with the tears that haven't slowed down.

*What have I done?*

# 38 - Jase

I pick up my phone, start a message to her, then close it out and put the phone back down. I've been doing this same dance for a few hours now. It's been over a month and I still haven't responded to A's text because I don't know what to say.

*How do you go from sharing every second of your life with someone to not being able to put a sentence together after months of silence?*

There's noise on the porch before the front door of the renovation house swings open and Jayde walks in. She and A couldn't be more opposite in every way. Jayde has never been here before, but she let herself in like it's something she's been doing for years. Ayla has helped me build half of the things inside of this house and she still would stand out on the porch and knock on the door, waiting for me to tell her to come in. Sometimes it strikes me how different they really are. Jayde is nothing like Ayla. It makes it easier to be around her that way.

Chris walks in a few steps behind her with a six pack of beer in hand. I still don't respond to any of Jayde's texts and try to avoid all of her advances, but she is always with Chris and I like hanging out with him. It's nice to have a friend that I can hang out with without all of the memories of A tied to him. I think Chris realizes that Jayde wants to hang out with the three of us because it's the only way she'll see me, but he seems to be okay with it, or at least, he's never said anything to me about it. And I'd rather pretend it's not happening at all, so that works for me. Jayde is around all the time, but that's the extent of it. I don't talk to her one on one and I don't respond to her texts or her photos because I don't want to give her the wrong idea. I've been pretty straight forward with her that nothing is going to happen between us, but that doesn't seem to deter her no matter how much time passes.

Jayde smiles at me and struts across the open hallway. She closes the distance between us quickly, like she can't bear being in the same room without being right next to me. She wraps her arms around me to hug me hello and I politely remove her hands from my neck and place them at her side. I nod at Chris as he hands me one of the bottles of beer and offers one to Jayde, too.

I silently notice the striking differences between Jayde and Ayla. Jayde doesn't hesitate and wait for me. She doesn't tell me what she wants or look at me with longing in her eyes. She goes for it, no questions asked with no fear and no shame. Even though I'm not into it, there's something about the way Jayde takes charge that I admire. I stare over her shoulder at my phone sitting on the counter and I immediately feel guilty.

I should write A back. I just don't know what to say to her at this point. Part of me is frustrated that she always seems to have the control. It's always about what she wants when she wants it and I usually give in to her.

Jayde takes a step forward and playfully pushes my arm to snap me out of my thoughts. I smile at her, but don't say anything as the two of them stare at me.

"What? What's wrong?" Jayde looks at me with big eyes full of concern.

"This feels kinda weird … " I start to say, and then hesitate as my voice trails off.

*It feels weird because this is my home with A.*

I've been building this house for years with the dream of us living in it together. We've made love in every room of the house. Every space has a memory of her and us together. I don't say any of this out loud.

Jade crosses her arms across her chest as Chris leans in close to her and kisses the side of her neck. She pulls away ever so slightly, frustrated with my lack of excitement of them being here.

"Are you kidding me? You're thinking about her right now? Are you ever going to get over her?! It's been months!"

Chris shakes his head at Jayde.

"It's not that simple, Jayde. Jase was with Ayla for years."

Chris looks at me with understanding and I smile at him gratefully, knowing that if I said anything close to that it would have sent Jayde into a tailspin. She's not a fan of talking about Ayla and makes that very obvious whenever A is brought up at all.

"This is always going to be weird for me," I say to the both of them. "Just being in this house with other people is weird. Let's go out — get a beer somewhere or something?"

I don't like having Jayde in this house because even though I know I shouldn't, I blame Jayde for Ayla breaking up with me. I think that if I went home that night instead of walking into the bar and hanging out with Chris and Jayde,

Ayla never would have doubted us. I know those are my mistakes to carry, but every time I'm with Jayde, that thought is at the back of my mind.

I grab for my keys and head outside with Chris and Jayde close behind me. The truth is, hanging out with these two helps keep my mind off of A. They are a distraction to keep me from missing her so much. They remind me that even though it's hard to conceive, life does go on without Ayla.

I avoid downtown and instead drive down long winding back roads to pass the time. Jayde and Chris continue to drink in the truck, but I keep the windows open and let the cool air fill the cab. It's nights like these where I think I can be okay. I stretch my arm out through the open window so I can feel the wind on my hand — so I can feel something… anything. If I don't think about A — if I don't have to deal with the pain in my heart every time her face comes to mind — I could be happy. These little moments make me believe it will be okay — when nothing else matters, when you don't have to worry what the future holds, when you don't have to deal with any tragedies, you can simply be in the moment and enjoy the company of the people with you.

My heart is constantly trying to convince my head that I should be with A, and my head is constantly trying to convince my heart that I should try to get over A. It never ends, but in this truck tonight, at least for a little while, I'm not thinking about Ayla.

But the second after I've dropped the two of them at Chris' apartment, I long for A's touch. I miss her smell and the taste of her mouth. I miss her smile and the way her eyes squeeze closed when she laughs. I miss the way she looks at me and makes me feel like the most important person in the world. The second I'm alone, my mind and body goes through withdrawal from her.

I'm stuck in this place where there's nothing I can do to change it, so I don't do anything. I don't take any action at all. I just try to enjoy each moment as it comes.

I sit in the truck outside the renovation house and my mind wanders to memories of A. I imagine her sitting next to me in the truck, smiling over at me and reaching for my hand. For a moment, I can almost feel her hand in mine and a slow ache starts its way across my chest. The second I get back inside the kitchen at the renovation house I pick up my phone and send a message to Ayla. I don't even think about it before I do it, my hands seemingly on autopilot.

*Sorry I haven't responded. I honestly wasn't sure what to say. I have been thinking of you, too, and miss you like crazy.*

# 39 - Ayla

I'm finishing a late dinner with a friend when my phone buzzes. I look down and see Jase's name and immediately feel lightheaded. My friend asks me if I'm okay and I tell her that I'm not feeling very well. She offers to drive me home, but I tell her that I'll be fine. I excuse myself and walk quickly to my car.

Once I'm inside I open the text with shaky hands.

*Sorry I haven't responded. I honestly wasn't sure what to say. I have been thinking of you, too, and miss you like crazy.*

Tears form in the corners of my eyes and I have to blink a few times to clear them. My heart starts beating rapidly in my chest and I have to take a few deep breaths to slow it down. I want to answer right away, but I have no idea what to say in response to that.

After a few attempts, I send him a message asking if I can call him.

*Hey – I'm on my way home from a late dinner. Is it ok if I call u when I get there?*

I put the phone down, but before I can even put the car in gear, the phone buzzes with his response.

*Sure*

I pull onto the highway with my heart thudding in my ears. I have been waiting for this for months, but now I'm shaking and nervous and have no idea what to say. The drive home is only ten minutes, but it feels like it takes hours. My palms are sweating when I pull my keys out of the ignition and I wipe them on my jeans.

By the time I get inside, my entire body is shaking, and my stomach is churning.

*Why am I so nervous? What is wrong with me?*

I realize I've been holding my breath and let it out in one long exhale before I hit the call button next to his name on my phone. The phone barely rings once before Jase picks up.

"A — how are you?"

Jase sounds breathless and I wonder if he is as nervous as I am.

"I've been good, I guess. How about you?"

*This feels awkward and I hate it.*

"Things here are busy."

Jase pauses a moment.

"I really miss you, A. I hate not talking to you or seeing you."

I look down at my feet and smile to myself.

"I miss you, too, Jase. I miss you so much," I say just above a whisper. "There are a lot of things I want to say to you … so many things, but now that you're actually on the phone with me, my mind is blank. I literally can't think straight."

I hear Jase laugh on his end. It's a sound that fills me with warmth.

"I wish you were here right now. I wish I could see your face while we talk. The phone isn't the same."

"I know. Me too."

I've waited so long for this. There are so many things that I've wanted to say to him for months. They all come out of me at once, like someone tipped the cup over and the contents empty in one big wave.

"Jase, I'm so sorry that I hurt you. That's the last thing that I'd ever want. I want you to be happy. I feel like the last couple of months we were together, I wasn't making you happy anymore."

I pause for a moment and am unsure of what to say next. My heart is beating so furiously that I can't concentrate.

"A, it's okay. You need to make yourself happy, too. I've realized in all of this that you need space to find your own happiness, and even though it hurt me to give that to you, I'm working on being okay with what things are now."

That's not the answer I had expected. I think I may have started this all wrong, but I'm not sure what to say next.

"Are you happy now, Jase? Are you happy without me?"

I try not to let the desperation I'm feeling show in my voice. Jase clears his throat before he responds.

"I'm trying to be. I don't want you to feel guilty. I don't want you to worry about me. I've been keeping myself busy."

"Yea, I've noticed."

I say it too quickly and with such bitterness that my hand flies to my mouth. I make a face at myself in the mirror in front of me even though Jase can't see.

"What does that mean?"

He sounds like he's laughing, but I can't tell for sure.

"Oh, you know, I hear things. I see social media posts."

I try to keep it light, like I'm teasing him, but the jealousy rings loud and clear in every word.

"A, come on. That's not fair and you know it. We're not together."

Jase's voice trails off and I'm not sure if he is referring to him and me or him and Jayde, but I'm too embarrassed to ask him to clarify. I'm not sure if I'm ready to hear his answer.

"Jase, I don't want things to be weird between us. I want you to be able to call me and it not be awkward. I don't want to feel uncomfortable calling or texting you, but I have no idea what's going on in your life now. I don't know if that's even possible."

"You can always call me or text me, A. It doesn't matter what's going on in my life, you will always be a part of mine if you want to be."

*I want to be. I made a mistake. I want to drive to you right now and wrap myself in your arms the second I see you. I want to kiss you and never stop kissing you. I miss you.*

I wish I could say all of the thoughts running through my head out loud, but I know that I can't. Tears are pouring down my face. I keep trying to find my voice, but I don't want him to know that I'm crying.

"Did I lose you, A?"

"No. No, I'm here. I know that you're realizing you can be happy without me. I've heard things about you and Jayde — that you are moving on and happy."

My voice catches in my throat and I stop abruptly, afraid to continue and make it obvious that I'm crying on my end.

"A, I know how hard it must have been to break up with me knowing it would hurt me, so there had to be a reason for it."

"Does Jayde make you happy?"

The question flies out of my mouth before I can think too much about it. The second it's out there, I regret it. It hangs in the air unanswered for a moment before Jase responds.

"I'm talking about us, A."

I hear Jase sigh and I can tell that I'm frustrating him. I put my head in my hands out of frustration with myself. I let jealous assumptions fill my head with every question Jase avoids about Jayde.

"A, nothing is the same anymore."

I sigh and nod in agreement, but I don't know what else to say, so the silence stretches out for a few minutes. When I finally do speak, my voice sounds strange and I'm unsure if it's because of the tears drowning me or the bitter taste of jealousy seeping into every word.

"The guys have told me that they haven't seen you this happy in a long time. It's always hard for us. It's never easy. I never made it easy. Between the distance and my issues, I feel like you haven't been happy in a really long time. But now you are."

Jase laughs sarcastically on the other end and I can hear the frustration rising in his voice.

"A, you have no idea how I am. The guys see me laughing and having a good time because that's what I want them to see. I barely hang out with them anymore. Like I said, nothing is the same."

I don't know what to say. Thinking about Jase avoiding hanging out with the guys makes me feel worse, and I didn't think feeling worse than I do was possible.

"Please talk to me, A."

Jase's voice sounds sad now and I let myself fall to the floor. I lay down with the phone and listen to my pulse keep rhythm in my ears.

"I'm here, Jase," I say softly into the phone. "I don't know what to say."

"I want you to tell me what you're thinking. I don't understand why you are jealous of Jayde. It doesn't feel fair. You broke up with me. I'm trying to understand, A."

"I told you, Jase. I want you to be happy. That's all I've ever wanted."

Jase sighs on the other end of the phone and I find myself imagining him next to me. I feel his hand entangled with mine and his warm breath on my neck. I close my eyes and try to remember what his fingers feel like across my skin.

"I want us to be able to pick up the phone and call each other and it not be so awkward. I want to be able to hang out with you when I'm there for Spring

Break and it not be painful for either one of us. I want the whole group of us to be together like the old days and it not be filled with so many things that make us sad. I want things that are impossible, I guess, but I want them anyway."

Jase is quiet on the other end of the phone for a long time and I feel like I once again said the wrong things. I can hear him breathing and it somehow makes me miss him more than I already do. I have the sudden urge to lay on his chest and listen to his heartbeat.

*Why is it so difficult for us to talk the way that we used to?*

"Jase?"

"I'm still here. I want impossible things, too. I'll try my best, A, but I can't promise that things are going to be the same because things aren't the same anymore."

We stay on the phone for a little longer. I don't think either one of us wants to hang up, but he finally says that he's falling asleep. We hang up, but he promises that we'll talk again soon before we do.

I lay on my floor for a long time after Jase is no longer there with the phone clutched tightly to my ear. The tears have long since dried along the sides of my face, but I'm afraid to move. Jase's voice made things better and worse at the same time. I ache for him every minute of every day and yet, I am not able to tell him that. I need him to go to the fellowship. I need him to follow his dream. I want more than anything to be a part of that dream, but I think he was right with what he said to me before I came back to New York. I have to find my own dream and my own path outside of him. I need to find a way to be strong without him before we can be strong again together.

I stare up at my ceiling trying to convince myself that everything will work out for the best. I worry that my heart will end up more broken than it already is. I can't seem to shake the feeling that I'm merely hanging on by a thread and one wrong move will sever my ties with Jase forever.

# 40 - Jase

I hit the button on my phone to check the time. I haven't slept all night and the sun is coming up already. Every time I try to close my eyes to sleep, Ayla's face comes to mind, and I find myself wishing she were here with me. Talking to her and hearing her voice made things better and worse at the same time.

Every time I think I'm slowly starting to get back to some semblance of normalcy, I think about A and my world comes crashing down at my feet.

I don't know how to be her friend and nothing more. I don't know if I'm capable of it, but if it's something she needs, I will do everything I can to make it work.

My stomach growls and I realize that I'm starving. I reach for my phone to text Chris, despite knowing that Jayde will be with him.

*Morning. Text me when ur awake. Breakfast?*

My phone buzzes immediately, which surprises me. I open the message.

*Morning, but I don't think this was meant 4 me. A little far for breakfast, no?*

I scroll up and realize that what I had meant to send to Chris I sent to A by mistake. I sit up in bed and text A back.

*Sorry — you've been on my mind all night so I must have hit your name instead*

I roll my eyes at myself and fall back on the bed.

*: ) I've been thinking about you too*

I blink a few times and reread her message back. I smile to myself. I picture A sitting next to me and envision her slow spreading smile that eventually explodes across her face. Everything else falls away. All the nerves and anxiousness about our phone call last night disappears momentarily. It's just me and A in this moment, the way it's supposed to be. I write her back.

*I wish you were here*

I reach into the dresser next to the bed and pull out a photo of the two of us that I had put away there. It feels so long ago, but I remember it like it was yesterday. It was a moment that Tate had captured in a photo, before anyone else knew we were together. I'm in water up to my knees and A is in my arms with her legs wrapped around me. She stares down at me like she doesn't see anything or anyone else. I remember how happy she was back then, before losing Tate changed everything for her — before she felt guilty for being happy and enjoying things. I trace my thumb along the edge of the picture frame as my phone vibrates with her response.

*Well, that would make breakfast a bit awkward for Jayde, no?*

I laugh out loud. I miss Ayla's sense of humor. I miss the way she can make me laugh so easily. She sends me another text before I can respond.

*Spring break is about a month away — wish I could fast forward time*

I immediately write her back.

*Haha – yea I guess it would. Can't wait to see you. A month feels like forever right now*

I put the framed photo of us back inside the dresser drawer.

*It does. Forever and a day, actually. Have fun at breakfast.*

I drop the phone on my bed and jump in the shower. I get dressed quickly and this time when I pick up my phone to text Chris, I make sure the message actually goes to him.

*Breakfast?*


A short time later, I'm sitting in my truck in front of Jayde's place. Chris told me that he'd meet me here. She's never ready when she says she will be and he's never on time, so I sit outside waiting in the truck. Jayde texts me to come in to wait, but I know better than to go inside without Chris there, too.

I open the messages with A from this morning and smile to myself. I can't keep my mind from drifting back to her.

When I pick up my head, Jayde is walking toward me. My stomach sinks as I watch her walk across the grass toward my truck. Chris is still nowhere in sight.

She's not dressed to go out, wearing a long white t-shirt with nothing else. Her feet are bare and as she makes her way closer to me, the sun shines off her dark hair and through the white shirt, illuminating that it's literally the only thing she is wearing. I jump out of the driver side and rush over to her.

"What are you doing?!"

She smiles up at me and puts her hands on the back of my neck. Her perfume fills my nose and mouth, choking me momentarily.

"Come inside. I have a surprise."

She winks at me and starts walking into her apartment, our hands linked between us. I shake my head behind her, knowing I don't want to be going inside. As we walk into the apartment, I see that she made the three of us breakfast and my heart sinks.

"I thought we were going out to eat?"

I feel trapped and I pray that Chris comes walking through the door any minute.

She has the small table set with three chairs. There's steam rising from the coffee mugs and a platter of pancakes in the middle. Jayde leads me over to the table and makes me sit in one of the chairs.

"Jayde, I need to talk to you."

She blinks a couple of times.

"Talk? About what?"

She looks down at me from her dark green eyes.

"Can you sit down, please?"

I'm losing my train of thought as she stands above me. She's making me anxious, but I want to say this before Chris walks in.

"Chris is my buddy and he really likes you. This stuff can't happen. You can't not wear clothes and invite me into your apartment without him here. You can't send me pictures or say the things you do. You just can't. It has to stop."

I clear my throat, trying to make eye contact with her, but Jayde bursts out in tears. Large, crocodile tears pour out of her eyes and she falls to the floor sobbing. It makes me feel like an asshole. I get up from the chair and sit next to her on the floor. She cries onto my shoulder awkwardly.

"Jayde," I whisper, but her hand shoots up and covers my mouth, stopping me from saying anything else.

She looks at me, tears still clinging to the corners of her eyes. She tries to reach for me, the desperation obvious, which makes me feel sick to my stomach. I pull out of her reach, but that only makes her sob harder. I look into her eyes and try to find the right words.

"I'm in love with Ayla, Jayde. I've never lied to you about that—"

Before I can say anything else, Jayde slaps me hard across the face. It happens so fast that I am in shock. She jumps to her feet and runs down the hallway to her bedroom, slamming the door behind her. I can feel the sting on the side of my face as I get to my feet.

The front door opens and closes at that moment, and Chris walks into the room where I'm standing, steam still rising from the mugs of coffee and pancakes.

"Awesome, she made breakfast?! Isn't she the best?"

Chris looks at me with a grin as he grabs a pancake in his hand and rolls it up. He takes a bite before realizing that Jayde is missing.

"Where's she at? Lemme guess. Still getting dressed?"

I look down at my feet, my cheek throbbing and I'm sure red from where Jayde slapped me.

"She's in her bedroom."

Chris walks down the hall and tries the doorknob, but it's locked.

"Get out!" she screams at us from the other side of the door.

"What's going on? Jayde, what happened?"

Chris looks at me in question and takes notice of my cheek.

"GET OUT!" she screams again, and I can hear the rage in her voice.

I look down at my feet again and shake my head, knowing that she isn't going to open the door while I'm there. I leave Chris sitting at the table set with breakfast and head out the front door. When I get to my truck, I can hear the sound of things being thrown from inside Jayde's apartment. I hear the crash of something breaking and a scream filled with anger. I get behind the wheel and text Chris from my phone while I'm still parked out front.

*Sorry, man. Not sure what happened, but obviously pissed her off. I'll leave you 2 to breakfast alone. Catch up later?*

My phone buzzes right away.

*No worries. I'm sure I'll figure out a way to calm her down.*

His text is immediately followed by a grinning devil emoji.

I shake my head and laugh to myself, but Jayde opens the front door to scream some profanities at me before slamming the front door again.

*Yikes.*

I'm not sure what it is that Jayde wants from me, but apparently Ayla isn't the only one that thought there was more going on between us than there is. I'm not sure what to do now, knowing that I won't feel comfortable hanging out with Jayde and Chris for a while. The truth is, I really miss my friends.

I send a quick text to Ryan as I pull out on to the road.

*Hey stranger, you up for some food?*

Again, my phone vibrates immediately.

*Hell yeah — it's been forever, bro. Pick me up?*

I start driving in the direction of Ryan's place, smiling to myself. I'm actually looking forward to Spring Break now instead of dreading it. Maybe it is possible that we can all be friends like we used to be. I'm just hoping that seeing A doesn't completely destroy me.

Thinking of her smiling at me in person is the only thing that makes me feel better, even if it's temporary, so I try to hold on to that feeling for as long as I can.

# 41 - Ayla

The music is blasting in my car and I'm singing at the top of my lungs when my phone starts ringing, momentarily stopping the music and leaving only my voice singing the soundtrack. I laugh quickly and look to the traffic on my left and right hoping that no one heard that despite having my windows down.

I'm on my way to Virginia to spend Spring Break with the guys, but I still have two hours to go and I keep hitting spurts of traffic, making the already long drive longer than it should be.

I'm frustrated and anxious to get out of the car, so when I see Ryan's name flashing across the screen of my Jeep, I'm thankful for the distraction of his phone call.

I click the button on the steering wheel to answer.

"Hey!"

"A! It's so good to hear your voice. What's the ETA? I can't wait to see you!"

Ryan's happy voice makes me immediately smile, even though I can see more traffic backing up ahead of me.

"I can't wait to see you either. I'm hoping to be there as soon as possible, but I keep hitting traffic and I am still at least two hours away."

"Yikes. That sucks, A. Well, I'm having some people over as a welcome home for you, and everyone is wondering where you are. It was supposed to be a surprise, but I've never been good at keeping a secret."

Ryan laughs and I laugh along with him.

"I will get there as soon as I can. Promise!"

"Okay, A. Just drive safe. See you soon."

I click the button again to end the call, and the music continues to blare through my speakers, making me jump in my seat. I quickly turn the volume down and ask the GPS to reroute the directions to avoid traffic. Within a moment or two, the robotic voice tells me to turn off at the next exit. I use my blinker to make my way over to the exit, hoping that this new route speeds the trip up a bit.

I let my mind wander back to being nervous and excited about seeing Jase, something that singing was supposed to be distracting me from. I'm worried that the second I see him, everything that I was feeling when I left will come rushing back — the ache of being without him, the terrifying thought that I've made a huge mistake, and worse, seeing him move on without me which makes me fear I've lost him forever.

I've spent so much time these past few months trying to gather myself because I unraveled a bit last summer. After Jesse and I spoke about it on New Years Eve, I talked to my sister about wanting to see a therapist, and she helped me find one that specializes in trauma and PTSD. It's never been easy for me to relive anything that happened the night that Tate died, but being able to talk to someone who's completely removed from the situation somehow eliminates a lot of the barriers that prevent me from opening up to everyone else. She's someone who I feel comfortable being vulnerable with, and she's helped me recognize that I need to take accountability for the things I can control now. She's helping me figure out how to do that.

Last summer, I felt frayed at the edges and constantly on the verge of breaking down. I was resentful and angry and bitter all of the time, and even when I tried my best to subdue it, those feelings were threaded through everything I did and said. I'm still working through my own feelings, but as Dr. Levin has helped me realize, it's okay to feel the things that I do as long as I find a way to cope with those feelings in a healthy way. I'm still working on living my life with the loss of Tate, which is something I've realized will be a lifelong journey. But I'm working on being okay with not being okay, with talking more about how I'm feeling instead of trying to hide everything and focusing on putting other people first instead of being so self-absorbed.

Dr. Levin has also helped me realize that I have to help myself feel and be better in order to put others first. I'm trying to do that. I'm trying to be clear headed and clear eyed. I can't even remember the last time I felt like I had to have a drink.

I shake my head, trying to clear memories of last summer that embarrass me. I'm ashamed I let myself get out of control, but the one thing that makes me feel better is that I'm working on taking the control back.

I'm worried that once I get back to the guys and the parties and the town where it all happened, that I'll go right back to a bad place, but I promised Dr. Levin that I will use some of the coping mechanisms she has taught me to rise above it — to be stronger than I was — but more importantly to recognize when I need help and ask for it, something I have always struggled with in the past.

I look down at the GPS again and it seems to be as confused as ever, telling me to make the next available U-turn, and then when I do, repeating the same direction sending me right back where I was. I'm beginning to get flustered and panicked because I have no idea where I am and no idea how to get back to the main highway now that the stupid GPS has steered me so far away from it.

*I guess there's no time like the present to start asking for help.*

I groan inwardly as I ask my phone to call Ryan once again, knowing the guys will never let me hear the end of being lost on a route that I've must have driven fifty times by now.

The phone rings a few times, but Ryan doesn't pick up. I momentarily forgot that he has people at the house waiting for me. He probably can't hear his phone.

I take a few deep breaths and call Zac next, but he doesn't answer either. The same happens when I call Jesse, and then Alex, Jackson and Mikey. I scroll through the numbers in my phone, steadily climbing to a deep panic. I pull over into an abandoned bank's parking lot on a back road. I can't even see a street sign and the GPS isn't updating. The small circle on the screen keeps spinning, which is exactly how my insides feel as my nerves churn rapidly.

Things like this shouldn't send me into a tailspin, but they do. Being trapped on a dark road in the middle of the night shouldn't terrify me, especially when I'm safely inside my car, but it does. I should call my dad, but I don't want to make him worry.

I take deep breaths in and out, trying to steady myself before I spin completely out of control. My finger lands on Jase's number and I press the call button just as an ambulance drives by, lights twisting and sirens blaring, which immediately sends me to another time and place and unable to catch my breath.

# 42 - Jase

"Jase, what are you drinking, bud?"

Ryan stands over an open cooler and waits for me to respond. I want to drink everything and anything tonight because I'm nervous to see her, nervous what seeing A in person will do to me, but something tells me I'm probably better off being sober and level-headed, just in case.

"I'm sticking to water tonight, Ry."

Ryan rolls his eyes at me and tosses an iced cold bottle of Dasani at me, which I catch one handed. He sits down next to me with a bottle of beer in his other hand and slaps me on the back.

"You ready for this?"

I look at him in question.

"Ready for what?"

"Seeing A … is it going to be weird for you now that you two aren't together?"

That's Ryan for you — always right to the point.

"Uh, I'm not sure to be honest. I'm hoping it's as normal as possible, whatever that means."

Ryan nods slowly, like he's agreeing with me while also deeply pondering what I said.

"You over her?"

His question surprises me, although I'm not sure why. I guess I'm just not expecting to have this conversation now, when she should be here any minute.

Before I can answer, Zac walks up behind us and slaps a large hand on each of our shoulders.

"Boys, tonight marks the last of our Spring Breaks together. Next year, some of us will be busy with real jobs or grad school and shit, so what craziness should we pursue this week? Better yet, what craziness should we inspire tonight?"

Zac grins and eyes us with a sparkle in his eye that only appears when he has concocted some ridiculous plan that most likely none of us will go along with.

"What did you have in mind?" Ryan asks, laughing at Zac.

Zac rubs his hands together and fakes evil laughter.

"Come with me, my friends. I've got a few ideas I'm working on."

I shake my head at Zac as both Ryan and I laugh together. I stand up with Ryan as we begin to follow Zac inside the house, but my phone rings as soon as I do. I tell Ryan I'll catch up with them as I pull the phone out of my pocket and see Ayla's name flash across the screen.

I walk quickly to the side of the house where it's quieter and answer the phone, my heart speeding up as I do.

There's no answer when I say hello, but I can hear sirens in the background, so I panic immediately.

"A? Are you there? Are you okay?"

She still doesn't say anything as I try to convince myself to calm down. I can hear her breathing into the phone, but it's rushed and heavy, like she can't catch her breath.

"A, can you hear me? Is everything okay?"

When she finally responds, her voice sounds small and very far away, like she's waking up from a dream.

"Jase, I need help."

I'm already jogging to my truck before she finishes her sentence, my mind racing with every horrible possibility. I can hear her crying softly on the other end and it breaks me. I try to keep my voice strong despite feeling like I can't breathe myself.

"Tell me what you need, A. I'm here. What do you need?"

I can hear the desperation in my voice, and I know she can hear it, too.

"I'm sorry … I'm okay … I'm just lost."

She gets the words out slowly with large breaths in between, like she's trying to calm herself down. My heartbeat slows a bit.

"You're sure that you're okay? What happened?"

I hear a few more deep breaths on the other end before she responds, but when she does, her voice sounds better — stronger and clear.

"I'm sorry if I scared you. I'm lost and my GPS isn't working. I'm scared and alone on some back road and an ambulance went by … "

Her voice trails off and I close my eyes, understanding setting in.

"The ambulance went by and I lost it. Trying to regain some composure here."

She laughs quickly — nervously — and I smile to myself.

"I'm so glad that you're okay! I heard the sirens and I lost it a bit, too."

I stay quiet for a moment, allowing her some time to get her breathing completely under control as I try to do the same on my end.

"So, I know I'm never going to live this down, but I'm completely lost. I don't even know where I am or how to get to you guys. I should only be about a half hour away or so, but that's hoping I didn't drive in the complete opposite direction of where I was supposed to."

Hearing her voice is filling me with all sorts of emotions, most of which I can't fully explain. I try to hide all of them from my voice.

"Drop me a pin and I'll talk you through how to get here. I'll stay on the phone with you until you get to a place you recognize. And don't worry, A. It'll be our little secret."

# 43 – Ayla

It turns out the GPS sent me in a wildly wrong direction. I was farther away from Ryan's place than I thought. When Jase nervously told me that I was lost in some small town more than two hours away, I almost lost it all over again. But as always, Jase was patient and calm and got me back to familiar roads so I could make the rest of the drive myself. I hung up with him when I finally got back to the highway, feeling terrible that I was keeping him from the party for so long, but making sure to thank him profusely before I hung up.

And now, as I pull into Ryan's long driveway, I recognize a few of the cars, but there aren't many here. Most people have left by now, heading on to continue the rest of their night at another party on the beach. I had gotten a text from Ryan while driving saying they were continuing the party somewhere else and to meet them there.

I park along the side of the driveway and turn the car off, not fully ready to go inside yet despite spending so many hours in the car. I send a quick text to my parents to let them know I arrived safely and that I hit a ton of traffic on the way. I leave out the part about me getting so lost and having a meltdown in some town I don't even remember the name of.

I get out of the car, but as I do, my keys slip from my hand. They fall onto the pavement with a loud clang that echoes against the vehicles parked around me. I bend down to pick them up, as I hear a car door slowly open and close.

*And there he is.*

Jase was sitting inside his truck and I didn't realize it. He stands in front of me, nervously shuffling his weight from one foot to another. Without thinking too much about it or letting anything convince me otherwise, I rush to him. I catch him by surprise as I wrap my arms tight around him. He doesn't hesitate and holds me close to him the second I start my embrace. I close my eyes as I lean into his chest and stay this way for a few moments, afraid that if I open my eyes, I will find that I imagined all of this.

Jase doesn't seem in a rush to let go either. I finally clear my throat and lean back so I can look at his face.

"You okay?" he asks me softly.

"I can't believe that I'm finally here," I say to him in a voice above a whisper. "It doesn't seem real. I've been waiting for this moment for so long now, it feels like forever. And then that drive legitimately felt like it took forever."

I smile at him, trying to make him laugh to ease any awkwardness out of the moment. It works and he laughs, squeezing me to him once more before letting go completely. I miss his touch the moment he does let go.

"So, bad news is, the guys all left to head to another party, but I said I'd wait for you here. Not sure what you're feeling up to doing, but if you're tired and want to head inside, I can always head to the renovation house instead."

He begins shifting his weight again and I realize he's nervous. I don't think he knows how to act around me anymore.

*Me either, Jase. Me either.*

"Let's go to the party. But do you mind driving because I don't think I can get back in that car again."

He laughs and nods and walks around to the passenger side of the truck to open the door for me. As I hop in and he closes the door behind me, I lean over and open the door on his side for him, something I always used to do and haven't done in quite some time. It makes Jase smile as he gets in. He stops for a moment and looks at me.

"I don't know what to call you anymore."

"What?" I ask him with a laugh.

"Well, you've always been Beautiful and I've always been Handsome, but that doesn't work anymore, does it?"

I think about it for a moment.

"I guess it doesn't," I say, my words not matching my thoughts.

Jase is smiling at me and I can see that he's trying to make me laugh.

"How about Gorgeous?"

I shake my head, trying not to smile. Jase laughs at me.

"Babycakes? Sweetheart? Cupcake? Baby Doll? Apple Of My Eye? Sunshine—"

Jase stops short, realizing what he just said.

"Sorry, I wasn't thinking. It came out before I could stop it … "

I reach out for his hand and give it a small squeeze.

"It's okay. Not Sunshine, though, because it makes me sad. And all of those are too generic. I don't want something you would call just anyone."

I wink at him as he laughs again. This time, it's his turn to squeeze my hand. He pauses for a moment, staring intently into my eyes.

"How about Ayla? I think we stick to that for a while."

I nod approvingly and let his hand go.

"That works for me."

Jase pulls the truck out of the driveway, and I stare out the window, trying to calm down everything inside of me that is screaming at me to kiss him. Because that's all I want to do in this moment — kiss him and never stop kissing him.

"What are you thinking?"

He's smiling at me and I remember that he can usually read me pretty well, especially when I want to be close to him. It's like an alarm that I send out unknowingly.

"What do you mean?" I ask him innocently.

"You've got that grin on your face like you're thinking dirty thoughts."

I know Jase is only teasing me and yet I blush anyway. He notices right away.

"You are thinking dirty thoughts!"

He laughs and reaches out for me, playfully grabbing at my arm. I steady his hand in my own and move to the middle of the seat, closing the distance between us.

"I know there are reasons that we can't be together, or shouldn't be together, and there are a million more reasons why this isn't a good idea, but all I can think about is you and me and my hands on you and your lips on mine. I can't think about anything else."

It's out of my mouth before I can think better of it. I don't overthink it or worry about rejection. I put it out there in the universe and wait for Jase to respond.

But he doesn't right away. The playfulness in the cab is replaced by silence, and for a moment, I wish I could take it all back. I look down at my lap and start to slide back to my side of the truck, but Jase's hand moves quickly to my thigh, keeping me right where I am.

"Don't."

I look at him, but he won't meet my eyes. His hand stays firmly on my leg, so I stay as quiet and as still as possible, not wanting to do anything that makes his hand leave my skin. We continue to drive, the only noise in the truck the sound of the keys dangling in the ignition every time we hit a small bump in the road.

I lean towards him very slowly, as if moving too fast will make him retreat completely. He tightens his grip on my thigh, pulling me toward him until I'm almost in his lap.

Being this physically close to him makes my senses come alive. I feel his fingers softly touching my skin. I can smell his cologne mixed with the scent of his soap. I look up at him and watch the way the corners of his mouth turn up as if he can sense my gaze. I look at his long eyelashes, the tip of his nose and the definition of his jaw.

Even more slowly still, I reach over and place a hand on his chest, moving up to the collar of his shirt. I run my fingers along his shoulders and then back to his neck, trying to memorize the way he feels beneath my touch.

I ask him only one question — one word punctuated with a question mark.

"Stop?"

There's no hesitation this time.

"No."

It's a quick, breathless, one-word answer and that's the only communication I need.

I lean in and kiss his neck, barely touching my lips to his skin. His hand moves slowly to my side, running his fingers along my bare skin underneath my shirt in small circles. His hand moves farther up, trailing goose bumps in its wake. I kiss just beneath his ear and then gently bite his earlobe, something that I know he loves. His hand moves out from under my shirt and hoists me in one motion onto his lap facing him.

"Please," he says, looking around me at the road in front of him.

I'm not sure what he's pleading for. I don't ask, though, and instead run my tongue along his skin. I kiss the side of his face, below his jaw and where his neck meets the muscles of his shoulder. My hands move to the bottom of his shirt and underneath to his warm skin. I run my fingernails lightly up both of his sides. My lips brush his ear.

"Pull over."

The words are out of my mouth before the thought fully enters my brain. Jase immediately pulls over to the side of the road. Wildflowers stretch out endlessly on either side of us and the moon is high overhead. His mouth finds mine as both of his hands move beneath my skirt, grasping the back of both of my legs. He lifts me up and lays me down across the bench seat, my legs wrapping around him as he continues to kiss me.

We don't take the time to get fully undressed, in a rush to feel as close to one another as possible. Jase's eyes never leave mine the entire time. I stare into them, watching them turn into pools of navy blue as I come undone over and over again.

# 44 – Jase

It's been two days since Ayla and I never made it to the beach party. I've been avoiding her since, and I feel like an asshole about it.

I keep thinking about seeing her in Ryan's driveway and the moment I got out of my truck.

*She stands up and turns around before she realizes it is me. I stop in my tracks, nervous, dumbfounded and slightly in a trance at the sight of her. Her hair falls around her face in waves. Her eyes are dark and sexy. All I want to do is gather her in my arms, but I'm stuck in place, afraid to move for some reason. She rushes to me, and I can't think in this moment. It's all action now — logic has left me completely.*

*Before long we are back in my truck on the way to meet the rest of the guys, something we never actually did. I'm trying to focus on the road ahead of me, but her hands are all over me. She kisses my neck and I pull her on top of me when her lips find my ear. She's driving me crazy, lightly kissing my shoulders, her hands trailing my sides underneath my shirt. Just when I think I can't take any more, she whispers for me to pull over.*

*So I did.*

*I'm entangled with her before the truck is fully in park, anxious to be as physically close to her as possible. My eyes never leave hers. Time seems to stand still, and I wish it actually would.*

We stayed in my truck on the side of the road for hours, talking and wrapped around each other. We used to spend so much time like this, and it makes me miss her and everything we had even more than I thought I could.

I dropped her back off at Ryan's house as the sun was just starting to come up, and I've stayed at the renovation house since, hiding from her and the rest of our friends. I know I'm hurting her by avoiding her, but I don't know what else to do. I can't go hang out with them like nothing in the truck happened, and I'm sure we're the talk of the town because neither one of us showed up at the party on the beach.

I honestly can't imagine what I'd do without my friends, but sometimes I wish they weren't as involved in my personal life as they are. So much of my relationship with A has been the topic of conversation among our group. Sometimes I feel like what goes on between me and Ayla is more like entertainment for everyone else. They forget that our hearts are tied up in this. I don't think any of them have had a serious relationship or have experienced what Ayla and I share together, so I don't expect them to understand. I get frustrated with it at times, and sometimes even miss the days where our relationship was a secret, something special that only we shared.

I know I can't avoid her forever. I know I can't avoid our friends forever. I'm just biding my time, trying to figure out how I feel about what happened between me and Ayla in the truck, and what it means. I haven't sent her a text or called her, but she hasn't reached out to me either, which means she's probably trying to figure out the same.

I know that this doesn't change anything between us. I'm still leaving for the fellowship in a couple of months, and she's still not coming with me. She needs to find herself or whatever it is that she's trying to figure out without me, and I need to focus on my future, even if that means accepting that my future doesn't include her in the same way that I want it to.

I shake my head, knowing that no matter how many times I tell myself that, it never seems to convince me. And seeing her only confirms that I can't control myself around her yet. Every thought in my head that night was telling me what was happening was a bad idea — for both of us. We should be working on severing those types of ties, but it's too difficult. Our bodies crave one another. I don't know how to go back to being only her friend. I don't know what to do or say. I don't know how to act like I don't want to hold her hand or kiss her, comfort her or hold her until she falls asleep in my arms.

My phone buzzes on the table next to me, a text from Ryan. I glance at it and know that I can't avoid them all week.

*BBQ at my place. No excuses. See you in 30.*

I grin at the text, despite my stomach dropping, because Ryan already knew I would try to come up with an excuse to not be there. He beat me to it. I shake my head, trying to get my mind straight before I head over there.

I try to convince myself that things can't happen between Ayla and me right now because we need to learn how to be apart from one another. I keep repeating that to myself as I get ready to go out, and I continue repeating it on the quick drive over to Ryan's place. No matter how many times I've said it in my head, everything in my body says otherwise when I pull into the driveway and see her.

She's wearing a white dress that blows softly in the wind as she stands still. She's drinking something in a green glass bottle. I watch the bottle move slowly to her lips. I close my eyes, thinking of her lips all over me the other night and I realize that I'm not strong enough to do this. I consider putting the keys back in the ignition and driving away before anyone notices when there's a loud noise at the driver's side window that makes me jump about three feet in the air.

Ryan is laughing at me through the window and I realize there's no leaving now. I open the door and Ryan steps backwards so that I can get out.

"What's up, Jase? Nice of you to show up, man. Where the hell have you been?"

As usual, Ryan is straight to the point with me. There's never any dancing around a subject with him, which I've always appreciated throughout our friendship. I look down for a minute, trying to think of how to respond.

"Honestly? It's really weird to be around Ayla right now. Weirder than I thought it would be, I guess."

Ryan's smile is gone now, and he reaches an arm up to grab one of my shoulders.

"Hey, you can't avoid it forever, Jase. I know you think I don't get it, but we all love you both and you're both part of this group of crazy friends we have. You guys are going to have to get used to being around each other. Figure the shit out. Man up."

He nods at me as he looks over the top of his sunglasses, waiting for me to agree. I know he's right, so I nod and smile at him. He uses one finger to push the sunglasses back up and takes a gulp of the beer in the same hand. His other hand reaches into his back pocket where he has a full bottle of beer stashed, opens it masterfully with one hand, and hands it to me.

I laugh, shake my head, and tip the open bottle to him. He clinks mine with his own and we walk toward the house. Ayla has thankfully disappeared for the moment, so I say hello to the rest of the guys without the pressure and awkwardness of everyone watching she and I greet each other.

We walk to the back side of the house where I can smell the grill cooking and hear a fire popping. It's just barely getting dark, and the wind picks up, carrying the smell of the steaks on the grill, which makes my mouth water.

I sit down next to Zac and Alex to catch up with both of them while Ryan returns to the grill. I can see Ayla just inside the house through the windows and watch as she tucks a stray piece of hair behind her ear. She laughs at whoever she is talking to inside the house and my heart stops.

*That damn smile.*

I keep repeating the mantra from earlier again, telling myself that nothing can happen between us anymore, even though I want it to with everything in me.

# 45 - Ayla

I stand in the kitchen at Ryan's, trying to pay attention to the conversation between Jesse and Ace, laughing when I think I am supposed to, but really what I'm trying to do is not look outside where Jase is sitting with Zac and Alex.

I saw his truck pull into the driveway not too long ago and went inside almost immediately. I don't know how to face him. I don't know what to say. I don't know how to act. I've been able to avoid seeing him for the past two days, but I figured he'd be at the BBQ today. My stomach has been in knots all morning knowing that I'd have to face him and completely clueless on what to say or do.

What happened in the truck the other night was unplanned and unexpected. It was like my body had a mind of its own. It always does around Jase. I don't regret what happened because I wanted it to happen. I am just unsure of what it means for us going forward. I know that Jase leaves for the fellowship in two months and nothing has changed for us. I still have a ton of work to do on myself before I think I could be someone that is good for him again. But despite all of that, despite what every ounce of logic is telling me over and over again for the past two days, all I want to do is go outside and jump into his arms like I always used to do. I want to sit down on his lap and feel his warmth against my back as we sit with our friends and laugh. I want to get in bed tonight knowing he's right behind me to hold me until we fall asleep.

"Ayla?"

I realize Ace asked me a question and I have no idea what it was.

"Sorry," I laugh, embarrassed I got caught lost in thought. "Forgive me. I was somewhere else. What did you say?"

"Ryan wants to know how you want your steak cooked, A," Jesse says with a laugh.

"Medium rare is good for me!"

Ace nods and heads outside to the grill to give Ryan our orders. Jesse looks back at me with a grin.

"Thinking about Jase I assume?"

I would try to deny it, but my face turns bright red betraying me. I shrug, looking down at my feet.

"This is all so very weird. I'm trying to pretend like it's not, but it is."

I look back up at Jesse and shrug again.

"Why would you pretend like it's not?" Jesse asks me.

"What do you mean?"

"What I mean, A, is that it is weird, and it's going to be weird. Why try to hide it? We all know it is. We don't expect you two to be best friends or anything."

I smile appreciatively at Jesse.

"That's true. I guess we're not fooling anyone by pretending we're both comfortable with being around each other yet."

Jesse laughs.

"No, you're definitely not. Now get your butt over here and help me with this salad."

I step up to the counter where Jesse is chopping cucumbers. The two of us always get stuck making the salad. It's become a tradition that the two of us continue, even though almost no one eats it. He hands me a cutting board, a peeler and a bag of carrots. I start slicing pieces of carrot into the large bowl of greens in front of us, my mind momentarily distracted from Jase sitting outside and grateful more than ever for my friendship with Jesse.

"You're a good friend, Jess."

He laughs at me but doesn't look up.

"I mean it. I don't know what I would do without you."

Jesse stops what he's doing, finally meeting my eyes.

"Ditto."

When we finish the salad, I know I can't avoid seeing Jase any longer. I step outside with the large bowl in my hands and place it on one of the picnic tables outside. Ryan yells over that he is almost done with the steaks as I grab a seltzer from the cooler next to the table. I glance around and realize there are only two open seats left, one next to Ashleigh that I know is intended for Ryan, and one next to Jesse, who happens to be sitting next to Jase.

I smile at Jase, who smiles back without saying anything, and Jesse moves over so the now empty seat is conveniently in between the two of them. I shoot daggers at Jesse from my eyes, but he whispers in my ear something about ripping the band aid off as I sit down.

"Hey," I say to Jase as I take my seat.

"Hey, A. How are you?"

"I'm good. You?"

"I'm good, too."

*This is super formal and weird and awkward. But at least we've spoken to each other now and that part is over with.*

Ryan carries two large platters filled with various cuts of steak over to the table.

"Those are all medium to medium well. The two that are basically still mooing are for Jase and A."

Ryan hands the platter to Jase, with our two medium rare steaks sitting on top. Jase puts one on my plate before helping himself and hands the platter to Alex on the other side of him.

It's quiet around the table as we all begin to eat, but not for long. Conversation picks up and stories and jokes are shared. It starts to feel like it always has. When it's time to clean up what's left of the food, Jase squeezes my knee under the table. I look at him and he asks if I want to take a walk on the beach with him. I can't find words, so I nod instead. We slip away while everyone else is carrying plates and leftover food inside.

We walk in silence for the first 50 feet or so before Jase speaks.

"This is weird, isn't it?"

I laugh, nervous and high-pitched.

"It is. Really weird."

Jase smiles and stops walking to turn and face me.

"The other night shouldn't have happened, A."

My heart sinks a bit hearing Jase say it. There's something about the way he says it that makes me feel like he didn't want it to happen, not that it simply shouldn't have happened.

I look up at him and he's staring at me, waiting for me to respond, although I'm not sure what answer he is looking for.

"I'm sorry," I say, sounding like a little kid who's in trouble. "I didn't plan on it, but things just happened."

I look down at my bare feet in the sand and wiggle my toes, afraid to meet Jase's eyes.

"I think we both don't know how to act around each other right now."

Jase's voice sounds weird, full of an emotion I have trouble placing. I can't tell if he's angry with me, or frustrated, or maybe just sad. I nod in agreement, unsure of what else to say because the million things that I want to say I can't.

Jase nods along with me, turning to look out at the water.

"I don't think I'm going to be around much for the rest of this week, A. And I'm leaving for the fellowship, so I won't see you until the end of the summer … "

I wait for Jase to continue. I'm unsure of the punchline so I wait for it despite knowing that it's going to hurt me like hell.

"A, I think being separate for a while will probably be a good thing for us."

*Yup, that hurt like hell.*

"You do?"

I'm surprised that my voice sounds strong and flat, completely disguising the fact that I'm dying inside. Jase turns back to me.

"I think we've both been on pause and waiting to get back together these past few months. What we're both realizing is that life continues to go on without the other person in it, and that's okay. But then we get back in this space with our friends where being together is familiar and comfortable, and old feelings come back. Being with you is like a reflex for me, something I don't have to think about. It just happens, like you said. I think me going to the fellowship this summer is for the best."

I nod, but not because I feel the same way that Jase does about us. I nod because he's right about the fellowship.

*It is for the best.*

Making sure he goes to the fellowship was what started all of this in the first place. I don't think he would have seen it that way if we were still together. Fixing me and saving me would have clouded his vision. It would have been all he was able to see.

I should feel good in this moment. I should feel proud that my goal is realized. But letting Jase go and realizing he's not coming back to me makes me feel more alone than ever. And I've never been good at being alone no matter how much I try to convince myself otherwise.

"I think we should make a plan for when you're back after the fellowship is over. We meet in this same spot, right here on the beach, and you can tell me everything about it."

Jase smiles at me, and I think I've offered him something he wanted or maybe needed to hear.

"I like that plan. I'll be back the first Friday in August."

"Perfect. The first Friday in August it is. It's a date."

"It's a date, A."

I smile as I look up at Jase, thinking about letting him go completely. I'm unsure if it's something I am capable of, but I will try anyway.

# 46 - Jase

There are days when I still can't believe that I am here. I glance around me at the other students in the fellowship program and I remind myself how lucky I am. I've only been here for a few weeks and I already feel like I've learned so much.

I've been studying Sam Maloof's life since I was a kid. My dad always admired his work, and I can still remember the very first time I saw one of his infamous rocking chairs. There was something about his style that struck me and stayed with me. From that day forward, I studied everything I could get my hands on about him. I learned that he was completely self-taught and his philosophy about art at the service of utility has always resonated with me, even as a kid. Basically, the form of his furniture always follows function. The Maloof rocking chair was the first time a piece of woodwork was featured in the White House collection of American furniture by a living craftsman and was exhibited at The Vatican Museum. I've read his autobiography countless times, so much so that the pages are curled from the many hours I lay in bed studying every page. When he passed away, I was devastated. But being able to work on the grounds that is now a working museum to his work and life is a dream come true.

His residence was relocated to a six-acre lemon grove shortly after it was deemed eligible for the National Register of Historic Places, which is also where the fellowship program takes place. Every day that I walk the grounds here, the scent of fresh lemons in the air, I think about how much Ayla would have loved this place. I wish I could have shared this with her. And every day, the soft ache in my chest reminds me that she didn't want to.

The goal of the fellowship program, which is funded by a foundation Sam founded with his wife Alfreda, is to continue Sam's work and inspire his philosophy within other artists and woodworkers, encouraging craftsmanship despite the popularity that machine-made products have gained. It's everything that I believe in, and why I put my heart and soul into everything I create. My work has evolved, even in the few weeks I've been here. I can see it changing and I love what I've been able to create.

But despite everything here that is making me feel like I'm coming into my own, like I'm finally finding myself through my work, there's always something at the back of my mind that holds me back. There's always a feeling that something is missing, because Ayla is missing, and no matter how hard I try, it doesn't go away.

The last conversation we had on the beach is something I think about often, looking forward to the day we return to that spot on the beach at the end of all of this.

I've met a lot of good people out here — people who love woodworking the way that I do — that can see what things can be instead of just what they are. I've made new friends and spend a lot of my evenings here socializing because I'd rather be out with people than home in the small temporary apartment alone. I've gone on a few dates with two different girls, one an artist attending another program by Sam's foundation, and one an aspiring chef who is currently the bartender at a spot near my place that a group of us visit often. I enjoy spending time with each for different reasons, but if I'm being honest, I'm only trying to distract myself from feeling lonely.

I miss Ayla and I miss home. I talk to my dad on the phone frequently, and he can hear the homesickness in my voice. He encourages me to extend my stay here after the fellowship is over, telling me he thinks it's good for me to experience new things before coming back home. I don't know how I feel about it. I wish there was a way to have home and here at the same time, but my life at either is so different from the other.

I had convinced Ryan to fly out and visit — he had a flight booked and everything — but he had to cancel last minute because of an important job interview. He felt terrible, but I told him there was no choice — he had to do the interview. Of course, he landed the job, and is now working at some big law firm part-time while he prepares for law school.

Everything at home is changing, and I know when I go back, it will feel like I've been gone for years instead of months. Part of me wonders if I should stay here longer and see if I can get a job for a few months. I'm sure I could get a recommendation from someone in the fellowship program or even work as an apprentice somewhere. But that feeling like something is missing is always there. I'm not sure I'll find whatever it is to fill this hole at home either, but there is something in me that craves the comfort of home and the way things were.

*I wonder if that will ever go away.*

# 47 - Ayla

This summer is strange and different, and not just because Jase is in California. Most of the guys graduated college this year. There is a buzz among everyone that all of the things they have planned for their future has to be figured out now — this summer. I feel left out, on the outskirts of everything because I still have two more years before I finish school, and I think I want to continue with other degrees after that.

I had so many plans when I was younger of what I wanted to be and what I wanted to accomplish, but that all feels so far away from anything I want now. Before Tate died, I wanted to produce large events and award shows. I loved working on the charity events each summer because it gave me a taste of that dream. But since life has changed so much and I've changed so much, lately I've been thinking about becoming a therapist myself. I like the idea of taking what happened to me and turning it into something positive for other people. My personal experience can help me offer empathy and compassion in ways others may not be able to. If I can help people who have gone through something similar or worse, then the experience can be turned into somewhat of a gift for others, and I like thinking about it that way. I'm hoping that continuing to educate myself will help me deal with my own trauma, and in turn, help me relate to what others have been through.

I walk to the front of the house as everyone else is getting ready for Ryan's annual fourth of July party, something that now has become a tradition and something that is always the talk of the town for weeks before and after. Usually, this is my favorite party of the summer, because summer still stretches endlessly out in front of us, full of possibilities. It was always a private celebration between me and Jase — the night we first kissed even though no one else knew it at the time. This year, there's no Jase and no exciting possibilities waiting for me — only days that feel empty loom ahead.

I am sitting on the front porch feeling sorry for myself when Jesse pulls into the driveway. He went to get ice for the party, and I regretted not going with him to pass the time. He hops out of his truck at the same time his passenger door opens, and I'm shocked to see Jake step out.

"Jake!"

I run to him at full speed and hug him as he laughs into the top of my head.

"Hey pretty lady! How are you?"

I step out of the embrace and look over at Jesse, shaking my head in disbelief.

"I ran into him downtown getting ice and I told him he had to come back with me. I wouldn't take no for an answer."

Jesse winks at me as he slings sleeves of ice over his shoulders. Jake grabs for my hand as I watch Jesse make his way across the front lawn.

"I hope it's okay that I'm here?" Jake asks me, waiting for my response.

"Of course it is! I'm so happy you're here!"

I walk hand in hand with Jake around the side of the house and into the backyard where the party is already starting to pick up. The guys all go crazy when they see Jake, and there are hugs and fist bumps and drinks offered from every angle.

"I feel like a celebrity," Jake laughs as he takes a drink from Jesse's hand.

"You know you love it," I say to Jake and we both laugh.

We settle into some comfortable chairs on the back deck and Jesse joins us after filling the coolers with ice. The night continues on and people come and go, but the three of us don't leave this spot the entire time.

Towards the end of the night, Ryan stops to sit with us and remind us that fireworks start in an hour. I thought he might continue on to another group of people and another conversation, but he stays seated with us instead.

"So, how're you doing, A?" Ryan asks me abruptly.

"I'm okay I guess," I say as I shrug.

I look nervously to both Jesse and Jake, but they won't meet my eyes. They are both looking only at Ryan. I start to feel like maybe this was planned. Ryan clears his throat and finally comes out with it.

"Listen, we're all a bit worried about you. You seem a little lost lately, and we just want you to know that we notice, and we love you, and we're here if you need to talk."

I laugh nervously at first, and then realize he's serious.

"Is this an intervention?" I ask jokingly, but part of me wonders if it is.

I look at Jesse, willing him to pick up his head to look at him. He finally does.

"You just ran into Jake downtown, huh?"

Jesse doesn't answer as I turn toward Jake.

"It didn't even occur to me that you don't ever go downtown anymore."

Jake smiles and reaches for me hand.

"A, you're not always the easiest person to talk to when it comes to yourself. If anyone else needs help, you're the first one there. We just want you to know that we're the first ones here for you."

I try to swallow the lump that has formed in my throat. I realize that while this conversation probably would have filled me with anger this time last year, it only makes me feel incredibly grateful now.

"Thank you, guys."

My voice is soft and low, and Ryan laughs out loud.

"Did you just say thank you?! No angry Ayla, just a simple old thank you?"

"I told you she's growing up. Our little girl is growing up," Jesse teases me, poking me in the side.

I punch him lightly in the arm.

"I mean it. Thank you. I'm really lucky to have friends like you."

Ryan is grinning that awe-inspiring grin of his and his dimple is out.

"So, while we're on the topic of you … what's going on with you and Jase? Has that ship sailed?"

Even though I know how direct Ryan can be, sometimes his words cut right through me when I'm not expecting them. I let a long breath of air fly out of my mouth before I can hold it back. Jake and Jesse are no longer laughing.

"Well, I'm not sure. I want to hope that we'll end up back together, but I don't know anymore."

Ryan looks confused.

"I don't understand, A. Didn't you tell him you weren't in love with him anymore? Didn't you break up with him?"

"Good question, Ryan," Jake says, placing his hands on his hips and looking at me. "Tell him what you did."

Ryan raises his eyebrows and looks at me, waiting.

"I lied."

My voice is low again and Ryan leans closer to me.

"What do you mean you lied?!"

Jesse cuts me off before I can say anything.

"She did what she thought was best for Jase. She knew he wouldn't go to California without her."

There are creases of concern across Ryan's forehead before understanding crosses his face. He leans back in his chair and steeples his hands together in front of him.

"So, you break up with Jase and tell him you aren't in love with him to make sure he goes to the fellowship he's been dreaming about since he was a kid, but break his heart and your heart in the process?"

I nod guiltily as Jake responds for me.

"That pretty much sums it up."

Ryan leans forward again, excitement back in his eyes.

"A, you have to tell him. You have to fly to California and tell him!"

"What?! I can't fly out to California now."

I look to Jake and Jesse for agreement at how crazy that sounds, but neither of them seem shocked by it. Jesse turns his head, thinking about it.

"Well, you could, A. We can book you a flight and I'll drive you to the airport. Maybe you should do it — tell him how you really feel and why he needed to go."

I turn to Jake who still hasn't said anything.

"And you, Jake? You think this crazy idea is a good one, too?"

Jake is quiet for a moment. He leans forward and places both of my hands inside his own.

"A, I think you have to tell him. One thing I've learned from everything we've been through is that you have no idea how long you have with the people you love. You should hold them tight and use every opportunity you can to tell them you love them. Don't take one minute for granted. Not one minute."

There is not one tear in Jake's eyes, despite mine filling with them. I can't argue with that because Jake is right. I got so caught up in pushing Jase away and feeling sorry for myself, that I forgot that lesson. I took time for granted, even though I promised myself I never would after Tate died.

"You're right. You're so right. What am I doing?! I have to tell him."

Ryan is fiddling with his phone for a few minutes before he stands up and leans down to kiss me on the top of my head. He hands over his phone, which shows a confirmation for a flight to California.

"Good. It's settled. Your flight is booked. You leave tomorrow."

# 48 - Jase

There are only a few weeks of the fellowship program left and I'm still unsure whether I'm heading back to Virginia afterwards or staying here. Life seems to have fallen into a comfortable, easy cycle. Everyone here is laid back and likes to go with the flow. There's no rush or pressure, even though I'm participating in a highly competitive program. Everyone is supportive of one another and the work. It's unlike anything I've ever experienced and I'm starting to really love it.

I'm celebrating at the bar with a group of friends from the program because we completed one of the bigger projects of the program, something we've been working on for weeks now. It feels good to have it behind us and know that we'll be completing the program in only a few weeks.

I sip on the whiskey in front of me and my mind keeps wandering to home. I have been trying not to think of Ayla lately, shutting out thoughts of her as soon as they start. It works most of the time, but I wonder if it's because I'm so far away. I wonder if everything will come crashing back once I return home. Part of me believes that's why dad is always pushing me to stay here longer. He's never been one to support running away from problems, but I think he understands that there's nothing that I can fix at home right now. Neither one of us has ever been good at accepting what is.

I pick up my head and almost drop my drink as Jayde makes her way across the bar straight towards me. I hop up from my seat.

"Jayde?! What are you doing here?"

She smiles without answering, sitting down next to me and signaling for me to sit next to her. She motions to the bartender, who just happens to be my friend, Emma. She raises her eyebrows at me as she takes Jayde's drink order and I shrug in response.

"Jayde?" I ask, waiting for an explanation when Emma walks away to make her drink.

Jayde leans back in her seat and smiles at me. She reaches her hand out and fixes the collar of my shirt, leaving her fingers on my skin for longer than necessary.

"You look good, Jase. You look really good."

I take another long drink of whiskey and let my arm rest on the bar in front of me. Jayde rests her arm next to mine, skin to skin, and I'm brought back to that night at the bar last Summer.

"What are you doing here, Jayde?" I ask once more.

"Just visiting, Jase. Had to come see you and boy am I glad that I did. Did I mention you look really good?"

She raises her eyebrows up and down at me and I can't help but laugh. It comes out before I can think better of it. She laughs, too, and I'm reminded what a beautiful smile she has.

Thankfully, Emma walks over at that moment with Jayde's drink and places it in front of her. She refills my whiskey without asking, telling me that I look like I need it.

*I couldn't agree more.*

I may need a few I think to myself as I watch Jayde's hand inch closer to mine on the bar.

# 49 – Ayla

My heart is beating so hard that I worry it may burst right out of my chest. I look down at the little piece of paper with the address that Ryan gave me. Jesse had dropped me off at the airport and the only thing that kept me from being a nervous wreck on the flight here was endlessly practicing what I was going to say once Jase opens the door.

I stumble over my own feet as I walk up to the blue door with the letters 3B on them.

*This is it. Ready or not.*

I almost lose my nerve and turn around before I take a deep breath and knock three times on the door. I wait a few moments and can hear footsteps on the other side of the door. It swings open and standing on the other side is Jayde, wearing nothing but a flannel shirt I had bought for Jase two years ago.

"Ohh."

That's all that escapes from my mouth. I stand there shocked, urging my feet to move but they don't. I hadn't prepared for this.

*Why on earth didn't I consider that a girl may be at his apartment?*

*How did I let myself get talked into this?*

*What the hell is Jayde doing here?!*

All of these thoughts jumble around in my head as I try to find words. I refuse to cry — not in front of her — but my voice and brain are both failing me.

"Can I help you?" Jayde says, grinning at me like the Cheshire Cat from Alice in Wonderland. "Jase ran out to get some breakfast. Did you want me to pass along a message?"

She stands there in only his shirt, filling the door frame like she owns the place. I close my eyes and when I open them, I spin around without saying a word.

My feet carry me the rest of the way to the street and I somehow manage to order a cab on my phone without one tear falling. My heart is still beating wildly as I get inside the car and ask the driver to take me to the airport. On the way, I change my flight home to one today and quickly text Jesse asking him if he can pick me up when I get back.

*What happened?*

When a few minutes pass without my reply, Jesse sends me another text.

*I'll be there. U ok?*

I type one word back to him.

*thanks*

I shut off my phone and bite the insides of my cheeks. The second the car pulls up in front of the airport, I run. I bolt through the automatic doors and rush into the closest bathroom and inside the first stall before I let the tears start. Once I let them come, there's no stopping what follows. Tears pour out of my eyes with no abandon now. I no longer care who sees or what they think.

I thought I was hollow, but seeing Jayde standing in Jase's door made me realize my heart was still in there somewhere because it exploded inside of me. I didn't just turn and walk away — I ran away.

I keep looking down, half expecting my heart to be on the outside of me. It feels exposed and raw. The idea of someone else getting to experience Jase the way I did makes me want to cry, punch something and die all at once.

*And for it to be Jayde of all people.*

A hot white rage ripples along my skin, electrifying each hair on end. But the tears do not stop. I have become the sobbing woman in the bathroom stall at the airport that no one wants to ask what's wrong. I brush away tears with wads of toilet paper and stuff them into the filthy toilet.

*This is your own fault. You did this.*

The bitter voice in my head reprimands me and I know it's the truth.

*You pushed him away so he could have what he wants and what he wants is her.*

One last lingering sob bubbles up and out of my throat and I clumsily pull at the toilet paper once more. Wiping away the proof of any tears from my eyes, I walk out of the stall and catch a glimpse in the mirror as I do. I pause for a moment staring into my own eyes.

*When did this become my life?*

The flight back to Virginia feels like it will never end. The second the wheels touch down, I turn my phone back on and see the barrage of texts from Ryan,

Jesse and Jake. Jesse must have told them I was coming right back. The texts range from worry and concern I chickened out to panicking and asking if I'm okay. I quickly text all three of them at once, feeling ashamed for making them worry.

*I'm ok, but*

I add the little broken heart emoji to the text.

*Jayde answered door and I ran. No happy ending — just end of story.*

There are responses immediately, but instead of reading them, I dial Jesse's number to let him know I landed. He answers immediately.

"A, I'm so sorry. That sucks."

This is why I called Jesse and not anyone else. Because with so few words, he sums it up without me having to say much at all.

"It does, Jess. It sucks a lot. Are you here? I just want to go home."

"Yea, A, I'm here. I'm right outside waiting for you."

As I walk through the airport doors to the outside, I quickly spot Jesse and rush to his car. Once inside, I don't say another word. He pulls away and onto the highway towards home, but after only ten minutes or so, he pulls into a rest area and parks the car. He doesn't say anything, but he holds me in his arms while I cry. I cry and I cry and I cry. Jesse holds me and doesn't let go until I stop.

# 50 – Jase

"It's good to see you, Pops," I say to him the second I catch him in the crowd at the airport.

We embrace quickly. It's this moment that I realize I made the right decision by coming home. The fellowship was an amazing experience, but it feels good to be home.

"Can't wait to hear all about it," Dad grunts as he pulls one of my suitcases from the metal carousel.

I grab the other and we make our way to the parking lot mostly in silence even though it's the first time we've seen each other in months. It's always been this way between us. Things that need to be said are said, and silence is okay, too. There's no awkwardness in the silence. I find comfort in it.

I hop in the truck on the driver's side as dad gets in opposite me. I had asked him to bring my truck to the airport so I could drive home.

"I miss driving this baby," I say to dad with a grin. "Everyone rides bicycles in California."

He laughs and slaps me on the back as we pull onto the highway. I fill him in on the woodworking projects I completed, even though I already told him about most of them over the phone. I tell him more about the friends I made and about the fellowship program itself. Before I know it, we're pulling in at his house and the ride home is over already.

"Pop, I'm heading to Ryan's for a little bit … "

"Abandoning your old man that quickly, huh?"

I look over at him feeling guilty as he gets out of the truck.

"I'm just teasing you. Go. Go have fun. Go see your girl."

Dad grins at me.

"How'd you know?" I ask him, returning the grin.

"Father's intuition," he says.

He walks inside, waving over his shoulder for me to go.

*I don't know what the heck I would do without that man.*

I'm heading to Ryan's house for one of his BBQs. I haven't seen any of the guys in a few months. I'm looking forward to telling them about the fellowship.

It's the first Friday in August and today marks the day of the date that Ayla and I set back during Spring Break, where we promised one another to meet on the beach and catch up. I'm not sure how to tell her everything I need to tell her. So many things have happened while I was in California that I don't know where to start.

Now that I'm sitting at Ryan's, I find myself nervous like I was when I invited her for pizza just the two of us for the very first time. I walk around the back of the house and the guys are in their usual spots on the back deck with Ryan at the grill. There are no signs of Ayla anywhere. I walk up the steps of the deck and they all notice me at once. Everyone jumps up and yells, and I'm instantly surrounded.

"Welcome home, man!" Ryan yells from the grill while I wrestle in the middle of hugs and shoves and slaps on the back — the typical welcome from this group.

I see Jake in the group and make it a point to give him a big hug.

"He's been filling in for you while you're gone," Jesse says.

"I don't know about that, but I've been hanging out more," Jake says, smiling at me. "It's getting a little easier to each time. I think it's been good for me — for all of us."

I pull Jake back in for a second hug.

"I'm glad to hear that, Jake."

And I mean it. He should have been hanging out with us all along. I'm glad it's getting easier for him to do so.

Everyone asks me about California. I tell them about the fellowship when all they really want to know is about the women out there. Ryan finishes the food on the grill and carries it back to the table where we're all sitting. We eat and drink and catch up. It's like no time has passed at all and I laugh about being worried that coming home after all this time would make everything feel different.

After food is finished, some of the guys walk down to the beach to start a fire, which leaves me, Ryan, Jesse and Jake on the back deck.

Jake's phone vibrates on the table next to him and he picks it up to read it. He stands up abruptly and announces he has to go.

"Everything okay, man?" I ask him, noticing the color draining from his face.

"Not sure. It's mom."

Jake takes off across the lawn toward his car and leaves. Ayla has told me a little bit about Jake's mom and what he's had to do to take care of her all of these years. It doesn't sound easy and I think to myself I should reach out to him. We probably have a lot in common when it comes to our mothers.

Ryan hands me a beer and sits down next to me. Jesse remains at the picnic table, which is only a few feet away. Now that it's only us, I ask what I've been waiting to ask since I got here earlier.

"Where's Ayla?"

Ryan looks over his sunglasses at me.

"Cemetery," Jesse says, his voice flat.

"Ah, should have guessed," I say nodding.

Ryan is staring at me and I can tell by the look on his face he wants to say something.

"What?" I ask him. "All of a sudden you aren't going to speak your mind?"

Ryan only shakes his head, but he has a weird look on his face.

"She's avoiding you," Jesse says, this time frustration in his voice.

"Jess," Ryan warns, but it doesn't stop him.

"You know, when you were filling us all in on the women out in California, you forgot to mention Jayde."

Jesse deadpans me and I realize my mouth is hanging open.

"How do you know about Jayde and Chris visiting?" I ask him.

"Jayde and Chris?" Ryan says, sitting forward in his seat.

"Yes," I say, looking at both of them like they've lost their minds. "They came to visit a few weeks ago. They stayed at my place before visiting Chris's brother in the next town over. Why?"

Jesse lays his forehead on the table in front of him and slowly shakes his head back and forth.

"Oh, Jase," Ryan says, still looking like he wants to say something more.

"Ry, what the hell is going on?! What are you not telling me?"

I sit all the way forward and pull the sunglasses off his face so I can see his eyes.

"It's A," Ryan says sighing. "She flew out to California to see you and Jayde answered the door."

I fall back in my seat like he punched me.

*Ayla came to see me?!*

"Jayde didn't tell you?" Jesse asks from the table.

"Uh, no. I had no idea Ayla was in California. I had no idea at all."

I close my eyes and try to imagine Ayla flying by herself to see me and Jayde answering the door when she got there. I can't imagine what she must have thought.

*I can't imagine what she must have felt.*

"Oh, guys, this is so bad," I say out loud.

"Yeah, Jase, it's been pretty bad. She's been a mess about it," Ryan says.

"Why did she fly to California? Why was she coming to see me?"

Jesse stops Ryan before he can say anything.

"She should tell you that herself. You know where to find her."

# 51 – Ayla

"Everything is so messed up now, Tate. I feel worse than when we first broke up, because as much as that hurt, there was still a part of me that believed we'd eventually get back together. Now that hope is gone, and it is crushing me."

I pause for a moment, missing Tate in this moment so much that it physically hurts.

"I wish you were here," I say out loud to the empty cemetery.

I've been spending a part of each day here since I got back from California. It's been kind of like therapy for me — a place where I can dump everything I'm feeling about Jase because it's too much for me to carry alone. I wish, like so many days that I come here, that Tate could talk back to me. I could really use my friend right now.

"I wish that I could have told him everything I was afraid of — everything I was feeling — before all of this happened. I wish I could rewind time before he met Jayde and talk to him. Why was it always so difficult for me to just talk to him?!"

My voice is loud, and it rings out across the field, yet again disturbing the quiet here. I clasp my hand over my mouth, a physical reminder to keep my voice down.

I fall to the ground with my feet underneath me and sit across from Tate's stone, staring at my shadowed reflection in the glossy surface.

"Why did I lie to him, Tate? Why did I tell him that I wasn't in love with him? I thought it was what he needed — what was best for him — and maybe it still is. But it's killing me."

My one-sided conversation is cut short by a small cough behind me. I jump in the air at the sound, my heart racing as I glance around me.

"A, it's me."

Jase's voice is quiet behind me. I twist around and he's standing ten feet away with both hands stuffed in his pockets, looking unsure if he should stay where he is or move closer.

"Jase, you scared the crap out of me!" I yell at him, a mixture of mortification for talking to myself out loud and fear that is always just below the surface of everything I do.

"I'm sorry, A," Jase says, and from his expression, I can tell he is.

"I didn't mean to scare you. I was waiting for a … break … in your conversation … before I let you know that I was here."

I groan inwardly.

*I probably look and sound like a crazy person. Hell, who am I kidding? At this point, I'm certifiable.*

"How much of that did you hear?"

I try to hide the absolute humiliation from my voice and fail miserably.

"I heard enough, A. I know you were talking about me and us. Is everything you said true?"

Jase takes one step forward and then stops. He looks frustrated and confused, and I don't blame him. This is a conversation that I wanted to start very differently, and now he's overheard parts that I'm not sure how to explain. All of the practicing on the plane fails me. I can't think of one sensible thing to say, but I try like hell to find the right words.

"I'm not sure how much you heard. I was rambling to Tate because that's what I do here."

I stop, questioning myself on how much more to say. Jase looks at me, waiting for more, so I continue.

"I was telling Tate how I screwed things up with us. I was telling him how I regret breaking up with you. I was telling Tate how messed up everything is now."

I say the last part as I stand up, taking a step towards Jase.

"I know this is all too late. I know I should have told you this months ago. I messed up, Jase. I messed everything up."

I look at my feet, afraid that if I look directly at him, I may start to cry. Everything in me wants to, but I think that will only make this harder for Jase to hear. When I look up again, Jase is standing right in front of me. He's so close to me that I can feel the heat coming off of his body.

"A, what are you trying to tell me? Are you saying you never wanted to break up? Are you saying you want to get back together? I don't understand."

I pause, knowing how unfair it is to say all of this now, when he's already moved on — when his heart already belongs to someone else. It feels selfish and I'm trying really hard lately not to be selfish anymore.

"I don't know how to answer that, Jase. I know that is frustrating and I'm not trying to be. I know what I want in my heart, but it's not that easy."

"I don't understand what that means, A. If you wanted to be with me, then why did we break up?!"

My head snaps up and I momentarily forget about Jayde — forget about her being in Jase's door in California — and I'm flooded with all of the fear and emotion that weighed us down last Summer.

"Because I was worried!" I say a little too loudly and too quickly.

I take a deep breath to calm myself before I continue.

"I was worried that we fell for each other too early and that we're heading in different directions. I was worried that we'll cling to each other because of everything behind us instead of looking at what we want for the future. I was worried that I've changed because of everything that happened with Tate and I'm no longer the person you fell in love with. I was worried that I'm not good for you and that I've become an anchor for you instead of a sail. Most of all, I was worried that you would stay with me because you are a good person and think it's the right thing to do instead of following your heart in search of the best thing for yourself."

The tears are flowing by the time I finish, and I can feel two continuous streams down the sides of my face drip onto my shirt before they silently hit the grass beneath me.

When Jase speaks, his voice is quiet and low. He reaches out for me, caressing my cheek and wiping away the tears as he does.

"A, why didn't you tell me all of this? All of these months I thought this was about you trying to figure out what you wanted. I thought you didn't want me anymore. You pushed me away so many times that it made me believe it. Now you're telling me that you did this for me — that you were trying to protect me from you? You didn't give me a choice! It's not always about what you think is best, because what I want matters, too! And what I want is you. If I get to choose, I choose you. I always choose you."

I try to regain my composure, but I'm lost in the moment. I'm caught up in all the time we've lost because I was too stubborn to simply talk to him about my fears. I take a few deep breaths and step back to look at him again.

"And I choose you, but I want what's best for you, even if that doesn't mean me. I don't know if I'm good for you, Jase."

Jase steps forward to lightly grab both of my arms.

"How could you not be good for me?! A, how could life without you be what's best for me? All this time apart made me feel like something was missing — like a part of me has been missing. The whole time I was in California I thought about how much better it would have been if you were with me. Every quiet moment there, my mind was on you and us and what I lost. I wish you would have told me all of this months ago. All of these months, A! All of these months we've been apart and the whole time we both wanted to be together."

"I know. I should have told you instead of keeping it all inside like I always do. I'm working on that and I'm getting better at it. I flew to California because I wanted to tell you then, but Jayde answered the door, and I didn't know what to say or do. I ran away like I always have — like I always do."

I try not to think of Jayde answering the door in his shirt, because it conjures feelings inside of me that I'm not proud of. I still don't know what it means that she was there or if they are together now.

"Jase, I'm not sure where we go from here? Should we continue to be friends so you can see where things go with Jayde?"

Jase is shaking his head furiously before I finish.

"I don't want to only be your friend, A. That's not what I want."

"What about Jayde?"

"Ayla, Jayde and I are not together. We have never been together. I know that you think I was interested in Jayde, but she has never been someone I want to be with. A, she's never been you. I have only ever wanted you."

I start to speak, but Jase stops me.

"I didn't know Jayde answered the door for you. A, I didn't even know you had been there until today when Ryan told me! Do you really think I would have let you leave California without talking to me if I knew you had been there? She never told me. She came to visit with Chris and they both slept on my couch. We got caught in a downpour the night before, and I gave them both clothes to wear because they hadn't intended on spending the night. It was a coincidence that it happened to be the same day you came to see me — a ridiculous and crazy coincidence."

I feel like an idiot and can feel my face fill with heat. I hang my head, thinking about how upset I let myself get and how I've spent the past month crying and feeling crushed inside because I ran away instead of finding out the truth.

"I've always wanted you, Jase. That's what I came to tell you that day and never did — that I lied to you when we broke up because I was afraid you wouldn't leave unless I did. The truth is I was and still am in love with you. But when I saw Jayde there, I thought that you were over me. I thought that you had moved on."

Jase finally breaks out into a small smile and he pulls me closer to him. He places both hands on either side of my face and holds them there.

"Can you say that again, please?"

I lean into his chest and laugh, thinking how strange it feels to laugh because there were times this past month when I wasn't sure I would laugh again.

"I love you, Jase. I never stopped loving you. I am in love with you now and I think I always will be."

He kisses me as I say the last word and it gets caught in our mouths, muffled by desire and the need to connect after all of this time. The kiss is long and full of passion from time lost, our hands pulling each other closer than our bodies allow. Jase finally breaks it, but we're both breathing heavy as we stare at one another.

"I want to keep doing that, and I will, but not here. Kissing you like that here feels wrong."

Jase grins again as I nod and smile, glancing over at Tate's headstone embarrassed as if he is standing there watching us.

"A, I love you, too. I never moved on. I've never stopped being in love with you. You're it for me."

I close my eyes and try to remember every detail of this moment. I open them as it starts to rain lightly, and I say a quiet goodbye to Tate. Jase reaches for my hand and leads me toward his truck parked on the hill, my free hand tracing Tate's name on his stone as we leave.

I think it's funny that Jase found me here at the cemetery — a place he has never felt comfortable but will now forever be the place where we returned to one another. I think to myself that Tate was part of that magic somehow, and that makes me smile and thank him silently.

# 52 - Jase

We make the short drive from the cemetery to Ryan's house, knowing that all of the guys will be in the same places I left them, but everything feels different now. When I left to head to the cemetery, my world still felt empty because A was not in it.

*When I left, I still only had half of my heart.*

Now my hand is entangled in hers and my heart is happy, but there is something I need to say to her before we go inside — before I lose her to everyone else and it's no longer just the two of us.

"A —there's something I should have said to you a long time ago — something you need to hear me say."

She peers at me through her dark, wild hair — brown eyes full of sadness and light all at the same time.

"Okay, but you're scaring me."

She squeezes my hand as I pull her closer to me, never breaking my gaze from her eyes.

"I know you've been through things that no one should have to experience, and I know you feel like it's changed you, but what you see as weaknesses I have always seen as strengths in you. When you talk about how you've changed since everything that happened to Tate, I don't see the same things you see when you look at yourself. You have an inner strength that allows you to always put others first, even when you are hurting yourself. Yes, you're angry, but that anger also makes you fierce when protecting those around you. And despite everything that would normally make other people bitter and resentful, you find a way to be compassionate and loving. You're figuring out how to be better through all of this, even if you can't see it now."

Her dark eyes spill over with tears and she kisses me softly.

"I love that you see strength when you look at me. I haven't been able to see anything but weakness in myself in a very long time."

Her voice is light and sad, but there's no bitterness in it. I place my hand underneath her chin and lift her head ever so slightly so that she is looking in my eyes again.

"Then I'll be here to remind you until you can see it again yourself."

We stay in the truck for a few moments longer, neither one of us wanting to leave this moment, where everything feels perfect and untouched by anyone else.

She climbs out of the truck at the same time I do, but our hands find one another again quickly, as if we've spent so much time apart and now our bodies can't handle being separated. I look down at her hand wrapped in mine and hope that it will always be this way — that it will always feel this good to be linked to her and know that she loves me.

As we walk together, hand in hand, into the house where all of our friends are waiting for us, I believe for the first time in a long time that it will be.

# 53 – Ayla

Ryan's family house still stands strong and proud in the same spot it always has, but no one lives in it now. Not long after the last summer we spent together, Ryan's dad decided it was time to move, although he never had the heart to sell it to someone else. Perfectly preserved memories and furniture lay under white sheets, forgotten and frozen in time. There's too much pain there. It lives in every inch and every board. It seeps out from the walls, keepers of the endless tears shed in their rooms.

Many years have passed, and many things have changed. Life moved on. We tried to keep our little group close, but life has a way of happening that makes it impossible to keep things as they were. Families and jobs and successes and failures — our lives were filled with them all — and that summer we spent here after the guys graduated college was the last one where we were all together. All of us except Tate.

My own life has taken me in and out of Virginia over the years, but when I'm here, my feet almost always bring me to Tate. More tombstones have been added with more names that you would recognize, but those stories are best kept for another time and place.

Today will always only be about Tate. Today marks the anniversary of the day he was taken from me — taken from all us. And despite all of the time that has passed, I still struggle on this day.

Some years, others join me at the cemetery to remember him, but today I am alone. That is mostly my own doing I suppose, but I've learned that regrets don't change anything you've done — anything you've said. You can only look forward and try to be better than you were.

I glance down at my hands as they tremor uncontrollably. It still happens every time my mind wanders to that night — every time I get caught in a cycle of memories that still feel so close and so real each time I relive them. This is among many things that remain a constant reminder in my life — my battle scars that never let me forget where I've been and what I've overcome.

I close my eyes and try to remember the self-soothing techniques that I have learned over the years. Sometimes simply closing my eyes and breathing deep helps calm me down and get my mind right. Times like these when I have trouble getting air in at all, it's easier for me to focus on my senses to ground me back in reality. I focus on the sun and the way that it feels on my skin. I listen to the birds chirping above me. I glance upward and count the clouds that I can see in the sky. All of these things bring me back to the current time and place instead of lost in a past that no one else can see.

This day always brings back the memories — a trigger for me that I can't control. Time moves on and the day comes each year, no matter how much I don't want it to. I've come so far, and I've learned to control most of it, but this day will always be a difficult one for me.

My hands have stopped shaking and I smile triumphantly at Tate's stone in front of me and the bunch of yellow sunflowers resting against it. Sunflowers have always remained my favorite flower, one of very few things that hasn't changed for me with time. It should be a memory tangled up with loss and grief like so many others, but sunflowers have always reminded me of sunshine and life. And this place could use a little sunshine and life. There's so much death here. I'm surrounded by it, and yet, it's still a place that strangely brings me comfort. For me, this place has been home to Tate for so long now, that by extension it feels like home to me, too.

Sadly, this is the last time I'll be visiting for a while — maybe ever, although I hope not. Life has taken another direction for me, leading me far away from this little cemetery in Virginia. I'm not sure that I'm ready to let go of this place yet. I've had to say goodbye to so many people and so many things that I hold tightly to anything that I can. The cemetery is something that I've always grasped onto for dear life, but now it's time for me to let this place go, too.

I kiss my fingers softly and run it across the top of his stone, trying to memorize every detail of this place so I can return in my mind when I need to. I walk away slowly, knowing that even in death, Tate has given me so much. He's been a listening ear, a source of strength and happy memories that give me light in my darkest times.

I glance back only once, as I push the heavy gate closed at the entrance. The familiar clang doesn't startle me the way that it used to, and I think back to the times when it did. I emptied so much grief into the grounds here — shedding tears, anger and frustration. As the gate closes one final time for me, I try to imagine closing the door to my grief as well but know deep down that is impossible.

I will always love Tate, and because of that, I will always be grieving for the life he didn't get to live, and for the life he did live with me. I've learned to be grateful for everything that has happened and everything we've experienced, even Tate's death, because each moment has taught me something.

And no matter how many years pass and age us, or how many things we've lost and gained, I will always be grateful for my summers away.

# Acknowledgments

First and foremost, I want to thank everyone who read Summers Away and patiently (and sometimes impatiently) awaited this sequel. It took so much longer to finish than I intended, but now that it is complete, I think it is better than I ever thought it could be. I am incredibly grateful for the endless support of the community of readers who loved Summers Away and who will hopefully love Summers After just as much. The characters in these books have become like real people to me — and I am in love with each for different reasons. I hope that you fall in love with them as much as I have, and that their stories bring you everything I experience while writing them — love, heartache, laughter, tears and hope.

There are also a handful of people that made this book possible that I owe endless gratitude to, including my cousin (Queen) Kelli, who was the first person to read the rough draft and who offered great insight into the characters as I developed many, many rounds of drafts. I also have to thank my mother, Roberta, both of my sisters, Krista and Kacie, and Larry. I don't know where I'd be without any of you, and I am grateful every single day for each of you. From reading drafts, to editing grammar and dialogue, to providing insight on where I needed to rework some of the plot and listening to me read chapters out loud so I can talk through them with you, I don't know how to properly convey how much it all means to me. Your love and your belief in me made this possible, and I will be eternally grateful.

Thank you from the bottom of my heart for believing in me and these books. I love you all very, very much.

# About the Author

Kara DeMaio loves to connect with people through writing, is inspired by everyday interactions between people and the role that relationships take in shaping who we are.

She strives to write books that raise awareness, encourage hope, and help open our eyes to the silent struggles we may not otherwise recognize.

Kara grew up in the Hudson Valley, and splits her time between New York and Florida. Her previously released titles include *Summers Away* and her debut poetry collection, *To You Love Me*.

To read more, please visit LifeTranscribed.com.